In Two Long Strides He Covered the Distance Between Them. . . .

Peter's face was white with fury as he swore at her through clenched teeth. "You'd drive a saint to Hell—by God." His eyes flashed and she felt as if black sparks were flying from his eyes into hers. "I'm sure as hell no saint!" He crushed her body to him and kissed her with ferocious intensity.

Hensley clung to him, realizing all at once she had neither the will nor the wish to escape from the exciting pressure of his embrace. She put her arms around his neck, her fingers touching the back of his sandy hair. As his mouth changed and became gentle on hers, an exquisite feeling of warmth caressed her like a summer breeze. . . .

FRAN WILSON

traces her love of writing to her grandfather but her love of romance is her own. A published writer of both fiction and nonfiction, she brings her knowledge of music, travel and Americana to these very special stories of people of today—in love.

Dear Reader,

Silhouette Romances is an exciting new publishing series, dedicated to bringing you the very best in contemporary romantic fiction from the very finest writers. Our stories and our heroines will give you all you want from romantic fiction.

Also, *you* play an important part in our future plans for Silhouette Romances. We welcome any suggestions or comments on our books, which should be sent to the address below.

So enjoy this book and all the wonderful romances from Silhouette. They're for *you!*

Silhouette Books
Editorial Office
47 Bedford Square
LONDON
WC1B 3DP

FRAN WILSON

Where MountainsWait

Silhouette Romance

Published by Silhouette Books

To my husband, Tom

Copyright © 1980 by Silhouette Books

First printing 1980

British Library C.I.P.

Wilson, Fran
  Where mountains wait.
  I. Title
  823'.9'IF   PS3573.I4569/

ISBN 0-340-26006-8

Printed and bound in Canada for
Hodder and Stoughton Paperbacks, a
division of Hodder and Stoughton Ltd.,
Mill Road, Dunton Green, Sevenoaks,
Kent (Editorial Office: 47 Bedford
Square, London, WC1 3DP).

Snow-crowned peaks that tower high
Heavenward and touch the sky
Serve as sentinels of fate.
Seek to know where mountains wait!

—f.e.w.

Chapter 1

"Hensley—Hensley Travis—what kind of fool name is that?" David Gillette's loud voice, accustomed to issuing assignments to a staff of newspapermen, filtered clearly through the partitions of his office. "O.K.—be it male or female, let me see it!"

Hensley, sitting just outside, shifted nervously in her chair. Waiting to see the editor of the Ironville *Daily Journal* in this male arena gave her the sensation of being the main attraction in a three-ring circus. She fingered the vivid green scarf tied at her neck, uncomfortable at being center stage while countless male eyes appraised her. Under other circumstances she would enjoy their flattering reactions, but now, awaiting her first job interview, they made her self-conscious. Deliberately she placed her hands in her lap, interlacing her fingers. Shifting her gaze from one side of the room to another, she tried to feign an attitude of nonchalance.

A short, slightly bald man emerged from the editor's office. Nodding in her direction, he beckoned with an ink-stained finger. "You can go in now," he said without enthusiasm.

Hensley stood up, tugging at her camel-colored jacket. She touched the collar tabs of the green blouse she had purchased especially to wear today, aware that this was her most flattering color. "Green sets off your hazel eyes," her mother had said to her many times. The vision of the emerald velveteen dress her mother had made her one Christmas appeared at that instant on the screen of her memory. She shrugged at the absurdity of her thoughts. Here she was, a college senior, about to have her first job interview and she was thinking, of all things, about a dress she had worn when she was a child of six.

David Gillette came from behind his desk as she entered his office. "Hensley Travis, isn't it?" he said, extending his hand.

"Yes, Mr. Gillette, and that happens to be a feminine kind of name!" She smiled. "And would you believe, also an unemployed journalist's name?"

"Is that right?" The red-haired man chuckled. Taking her slender hand in a firm grasp, he shook it warmly. "I guess you couldn't fail to hear this loud mouth of mine sounding off, now, could you? You must admit, however, that Hensley Travis is hardly a name a man would associate with such a pretty girl as you!" His laughing blue eyes scrutinized her from behind large metal-rimmed glasses. "Now, have a seat here by my desk and tell me what it is I can do for you."

She liked the glib informality of his manner. "I want a job, Mr. Gillette," she said eagerly. "I'm graduating next month and I hope to go to work on your newspaper. I can write. In fact, I'm a good writer," she added, hoping she sounded sure of herself. "I received the Lakeland Award in journalism this year!"

"Hum—the Lakeland, eh . . ." Removing his glasses, he held them in his right hand and wagged them at her. "Speaks well for you. I know how competitive that award is."

His words increased her confidence. She now handed

him the manila folder she had been holding on her lap. "I brought some copy I did for our college paper." .

David replaced his glasses and took the folder. Rummaging through the clutter of papers on his desk, he located a wide black pencil, which he positioned under each sentence as he read. Hensley leaned back in her chair, her lips pressed together in silence.

David chuckled. "Uh-huh—pretty good . . ." he mumbled without looking up. Hensley's tensions eased. As David continued reading, she took the opportunity to study this newspaperman with his strident voice. He had unruly red hair, the same shade as the coat of an Irish setter. The smattering of freckles that saddled his nose gave him a youthful appearance. They did not, however, camouflage the fine lines that traced his forehead and edged his steel-blue eyes. She seldom gave much thought to age in men. Outside of her contemporaries, she pushed all men into two categories. Over fifty was her father's group, and otherwise they fell in with her brother, Allan, who was thirty-two. She did wonder, however, how old the eidtor of Ironville, Minnesota's only newspaper might be. Probably, she imagined, he was about ten years older than Allan, but no matter what his age, there was a magnetic quality about David Gillette.

He looked up, and Hensley quickly turned her eyes away from his, her face reddening. She felt embarrassed to be caught studying him so intently. He appeared, however, to take no notice. Closing the manila folder, he tapped it on the top of his desk to align the contents.

"This is good work," he said, rubbing his forehead.

She smiled, really pleased by his words.

David appeared to consider her thoughtfully. "I'll tell you frankly, I'm not interested in baby-sitting a starry-eyed journalism student with a new diploma in her hand."

She drew in her breath in a gasp, the former second

9

of pleasure destroyed, her small hoard of confidence disintegrating at his words.

"I hope you won't think I have anything against women in the media," he added. Pulling off his glasses, he placed them on top of the papers on his desk.

Hensley pressed her trembling hands together in her lap. "I guess you might say I'm 'starry-eyed' about journalism, Mr. Gillette," she managed to say lightly. "But you did also say you thought my work was good," she added, her voice firm.

"I did. I meant it too, but I run into a number of people like you, all wanting to get their feet wet in the inky sea of newspaper print. I'm afraid I'm not an editor who has the time or patience to keep them from drowning!"

Angered by his words, she straightened her shoulders and looked directly at him. "That's not a fair attitude," she said. "Give me a chance. I'll show you! I'll swim through your inky sea and I'll make the final edition!"

David threw back his head in laughter. "I like your style, Hensley Travis. I've told you I expect top performance from my people. O.K."—he was looking her squarely in the eye now—"with this understanding: I will take you on a trial basis. Three months—no promise of anything more unless you deliver the caliber of work I demand. If that interests you, you may come to work here the first of June."

She grinned. "You bet it interests me, Mr. Gillette!" She tingled with exhilaration. She had a job! How surprised Allan would be when she told him. She pushed her hair back from her flushed face.

"Hensley?" David's voice comanded her attention. "I see here you've listed only your college address." He was penciling notes on her job-application form. "I need your Ironville address. You're home is here, isn't it?"

She nodded, then paused and shook her head. "I'm sort of in limbo." She gave a self-conscious laugh. "Kind of adrift, you might say. I'll be staying at my brother's apartment here this summer. I'd better explain. You see, I lived with my father in the president's house on the campus, but after he died last year, I moved into the dorm. I really haven't had a permanent home since Dad's been gone."

"I'll be damned!" David slapped his chair arm in surprise. "You're father was Franklin Travis, president of the university—what do you know! I should have put you together with the Travis name." Smiling, he leaned back, and taking a package of cigarettes from his shirt pocket, he offered her one. She shook her head.

"Did you know my father?" she questioned him eagerly.

"Not well, but we were acquainted." David salvaged a lighter from the clutter on his desk to light a cigarette. "Fact is, we shared an interest in stamp collecting. I remember some years ago at the International Philatelists Convention, I had quite a conversation with your father about some rare Canadian stamps he owned—all perfect pairs they were!" He grinned at her. "God! How I did envy him those stamps. Particularly the ten-penny blue set of the explorer Jacques Cartier. Jewel of a stamp, that one." He pulled a large amber ashtray into closer range as he spoke. "Worth twenty-five hundred dollars on the current market, I'll bet you!"

Hensley shifted her position slightly to escape the path of his cigarette smoke. "You make me feel as if I should take the time to learn about stamp collecting, but I'm afraid I'm not into that." She shrugged. "I feel, if you don't want to put it on a letter and mail it, why have it at all?" She hesitated, wondering if she had said the wrong thing. After all, she should not appear flippant with her new boss.

"Let me tell you something," he said, pointing his finger at her. "I'd give anything to purchase that Cartier stamp. And don't you forget it! If you're ever in the mood to sell it, you just let me know!"

"You'll have to speak to my brother about that, Mr. Gillette. Allan is the stamp collector in the family now, and he considers Dad's collection a kind of family legacy." She stood up, feeling it was probably time for her to leave.

"Good man, and he's right too!" David agreed. "That entire Canadian series has a catalog value in excess of fifty thousand dollars—not a bad legacy!" Coming from behind his desk, he walked with Hensley to the doorway. "Well, Hensley, I'll harangue you further about buying your father's stamps when you're working here at the *Journal*." He laughed warmly. "See you the first day of June."

She walked through the outer office, this time enjoying the admiring glances of the staff. Once outside the building, she crossed her arms, hugging herself in a feeling of achievement. She had gotten a job without help from anyone, strictly on her own merit. Not because she was President Travis' daughter or Allan Travis' sister, but because she was herself—Hensley Travis. Mimicking David Gillette, she said aloud, "Hensley Travis—what kind of fool name is that?" A woman walking toward her on the sidewalk stared goggle-eyed at Hensley and then quickened her steps. Flinging her head back, Hensley suppressed her laughter and walked in a decorous manner to her car.

Traffic was steady on the boulevard, more than usual for a quarter to four in the afternoon, she thought. She was a competent driver; still, throbbing motors and the hum of speeding tires plagued Hensley with uneasiness. She had been in the car the day her mother had been killed. It had been on a fast, well-traveled avenue such

12

as this. Although the accident had occurred almost twelve years ago, it remained vivid in her memory. She ran the tip of her tongue across her upper lip, touched with sadness as she thought of her mother for the second time this afternoon. She glanced at the Minnesota evergreens that lined the residential street she entered as she left the boulevard. They were the same rich shade of green as the velveteen of her Christmas dress.

At the end of the next block she turned and drove into the parking area at her brother's apartment complex. She noticed the stall reserved for his car was empty. Well, it was early yet. He'd be along soon. Parking in the area designated for visitors, she locked her car and hurried along the protected walkway to her brother's first-floor apartment. Flipping through the keys on her key ring, she singled out the one she needed. Although she rarely drove the seventy miles from school without first calling ahead, she had on occasion, as today, been unable to reach Allan by telephone before leaving the campus. On an earlier occasion she had come down on a Friday afternoon to find Allan away for the weekend, and she had been forced to turn around and return to school. After this happened, Allan had an extra key made for her.

Now, as she entered, she found it cold and airless. Obviously the place had been closed for several days; it had that unlived-in smell and feel. She wrinkled her nose in distaste. She wondered where Allan could have gone. She knew that the mining firm he represented kept him at the site of the open-pit iron mines in the Mesabi Range for part of each month. But she also knew that since his illness, his trips had been less frequent.

Tossing her purse on the coffee table, she crossed to the windows, opening the draperies to allow the bright splashes of April sun to dispel the gloom. Shivering, she hugged herself against the chill and turned the dial setting on the thermostat until she heard the familiar click as the heat came on. The emptiness of the room depressed her and the addition of sunlight and heat did little to lessen her disappointment at not finding Allan here. She had counted on barging in and amazing him with her news of getting a job. She let out a sigh, for she had also schemed to get Allan to take her to the Wagon Wheel for dinner so she could hear that good country-western duo that performed there on weekends. Absently she twisted the scarf at her neck. If Allan had been at the Mesabi Range all week, he would certainly be home later this evening. It was Friday. He always got home on the weekend. She pushed her hair behind her ears. Regardless of when Allan might arrive, she certainly had no intention of driving back to the university tonight.

Aimlessly she headed into the kitchen. Opening the refrigerator, she found the contents uninteresting. There were no perishables other than a partial pound of bacon, which though wrapped in two layers of plastic appeared dried out and gray in color. A jar of pickles, one of mustard and one of mayonnaise nestled at one side of a shelf. A container of powdered creamer stood isolated in the opposite corner. Hensley grimaced at these unappetizing bachelor staples. Fortunately the door rack held three bottles of soda. Darn, it did appear that Allan had planned on being away for a while. Where might he be? Surely he was feeling all right? He would let her know if he were really sick again, wouldn't he? She chewed her lip. She was letting the emptiness of the apartment get to her.

Lifting out a bottle of soda, she reached with the other hand to pull a tray of ice from the freezer compartment. Nudging the top freezer door shut with her head and one shoulder, she shoved the lower door with an elbow and hip, managing the operation as if she were performing a rhythmic bump and roll. Preoccupied with these gyrations, she failed to hear the key turn in the door lock.

"Allan!" a voice called out. "Allan, are you here?"

Startled, Hensley let the aluminium ice tray slip from her hand, and ice cubes pelted the sink in a brittle staccato rhythm.

"Oh! What happened? Did you break something?"

Hensley heard the words and then a dark-haired girl in red slacks and a white pullover blouse appeared in the open doorway to the kitchen. The strange girl stared at Hensley, her green eyes fluttering like a frightened doe catching sight of a predatory enemy.

"I . . . I thought Allan was in here. I'm looking for him," she said, bracing herself against the door frame. "I . . . I'm sorry if I startled you." She blinked her eyes as if to escape Hensley's intent gaze, a flush of embarrassment coloring her ivory skin.

"We really did surprise each other, didn't we?" Hensley gave a nervous laugh. She tried to recall if she had ever seen this girl before, knowing, almost instinctively, that she had not. She would certainly remember such a cameo-perfect face. "The truth is, I'm looking for Allan too. I was surprised this afternoon when I found the apartment cold and deserted. My guess is he's probably been away all week. Do you know where he went?" Hensley smiled, adding quickly, "I'm Allan's sister, Hensley—or hadn't you guessed that?"

The girl's round eyes began to sparkle and Hensley enjoyed watching her pleased reaction. "Oh, you're Hensley! Oh!" She smiled. "Well, I guess there's no point in my denying that I'm relieved to hear that!" She hesitated and Hensley heard her quick intake of breath before she added, "I'm glad you're not a new girl of Allan's. Although, if I were a fair person, I should have hoped you were."

Hensley gaped, not knowing how to respond to her. The girl's sudden deliberate manner mystified her. "Since we both are waiting for my brother, let's have a soda," Hensley blurted into the gap of silence between them. "He'll surely be here shortly." She reached for two glasses and began to fill them with ice cubes.

"No—I can't wait. Thank you, but I really won't stay to see him. I guess it's not all that important anyway." She hesitated a minute, then turned and left the kitchen. In that instant Hensley could swear she saw tears hovering in her green eyes.

"Wait—please!" Hensley called after her. "I want to tell Allan you were here! Wait—I don't even know your name." She hurried after her, but the stranger fled, leaving the door ajar. Hensley watched as the girl ran along the covered walkway and disappeared around the corner of the building.

Shaking her head, she stepped back inside the apartment, closing the door. Turning, she saw her confused expression reflected in the hall mirror. It was then she caught sight of the key. On the narrow half-circle table beneath the entry-hall mirror lay a brass door key. Picking it up, she turned it over slowly in her hand. The metal felt cold. She did not need to really examine it, nor was it necessary to actually compare it with the one Allan had given her. She knew they were alike. She knew, too, that it had to be the key the unnamed girl had used to enter Allan's apartment. A shiver of apprehension touched her. The key seemed suddenly heavy, like iron in her hand.

Why would a girl who possessed a key to Allan's apartment not know where he was? Wouldn't he have told her if he were leaving town, when he would return? None of this made any sense!

She tossed her head, determined to speculate no further. Placing the brass key on the console table where the girl had left it, she went back to the kitchen and poured herself a soda. Returning to the living room, she eased down on the sofa, absently studying the embossed pattern of the light gold carpet. All her earlier feelings of exhilaration over her new job had faded. Lonely and anxious, she desperately wished the front door would swing open and Allan would be there. She raised her eyes, staring ahead—as if wanting it could make it happen. But the closed door, the empty hall, stared back at her in silence.

Chapter 2

"Good morning, Emma," Peter Merrick greeted his secretary as he strode into the office. "Has John Martin called from the smeltery this morning?"

"No, he hasn't. Would you like me to call him?" She laid her hand on the telephone on her desk, as if she knew his answer before he gave it.

"Yes, do that!" His eyes met those of the competent gray-haired woman. "You're one step ahead of me already this morning, as usual," he said. He smiled, thinking that Emma Carlson was such an integral part of the Merrick Copper Company it was not at all surprising that she anticipated his reactions. She had been his father's secretary for twenty-three years prior to his death. Certainly Emma had eased the transition for him when he took over the reins of the company four years ago.

"Tell John I need to get together with him on the ecological changes to be carried out at the smelteries. Better set up a meeting before noon. With Allan Travis due to arrive late this afternoon, I don't want anything of importance hanging fire!" Pausing at the door to his private office, Peter added, "Clear me from three o'clock on today, Emma. Regardless of what Allan said on the phone about a leisurely drive out, I know the ol' miner. There'll be no holding him once he crosses the state line into Montana." Peter chuckled. "He'll race his motor the rest of the way into Anaconda. And I damn sure want to be out at the ranch to meet him!"

Entering his office, he took off his coat, hanging it over one of the chairs that flanked the long library table at the end of the room. Geological maps, rolled and stacked like a giant honeycomb, lay centered on the table. Peter crossed to his desk and picked up his pipe. Holding the bowl in his hand, he made no move to fill it. His mind was still occupied with thoughts of Allan. Peter doubted that his friend was physically up to making this trip by car, yet when he had suggested on the phone that Allan take the plane there had been stubborn rejection.

"I want another chance to see all that western scenery of yours, Pete," he had declared. "One of the reasons for my coming is to see those mountains one more time! I miss the sight of them."

Peter had caught the note of nostalgia in Allan's voice. "See the mountains—one more time," he had said. Peter frowned. Uneasy speculation sandpapered cross-grain in his mind.

God knows, there was no one on earth Peter would rather see, but there was something wrong about the timing of this visit—unseasonable. Ever since their college days, he and Allan had arranged to get together twice a year. But it was lake fishing in Minnesota in the summer and a week of midwinter skiing at Big Sky here in Montana. Peter recalled the exchange of letters each time to make plans for these get-togethers—not like this time at all! No—five days ago when Allan phoned from Ironville, there had been an undercurrent of urgency in his need to come out at this particular time. There had been something about Allan having to get back to Minnesota for Hensley's graduation in May. That bit had seemed curious to Peter. What could his sister's college graduation in May have to do with Allan needing to make the trip in April? Well, he'd soon know the answer. He did wish Allan had waited and come when he could stay longer—four or five days was a damn short visit.

He swiveled his chair so he could reach the bookshelves behind his desk. Removing the lid from the copper humidor that rested at one side of the lower shelf, he filled his pipe with the rich blend of tobacco. Emma, bless her, made certain that the humidor was always filled with his favorite aromatic mixture.

As wisps of smoke curled around the pipe stem, the set lines of Peter's jaw relaxed. He began to feel easier with his thoughts. Allan had, after all, sounded darn good on the phone. He smiled, recalling what Allan had said about Hensley.

"That impulsive and impressionable sister of mine is a major reason for my coming," he had said. "I hope you can help me with some plans for her." Allan had laughed that deep-throated laugh of his and added, "Wait until you hear her latest! She's into country-rock music with all-out enthusiasm, the way she tackles everything." He laughed again. "When she's at my apartment, she insists on listening to country albums day and night. When I complain, she threatens to buy a guitar and take lessons. Hensley would do it, too, so I can't win!"

"Impulsive and impressionable"—Peter could certainly buy that! He remembered what a brash teenager Hensley had been—long legs and long blond hair. He grinned, thinking of when he and Allan had graduated from Montana University nine years ago. Hensley had been thirteen. At the ceremonies, she had worn huge green sunglasses—*shades* she had called them. She wore them constantly, refusing to remove them even indoors, claiming they had something to do with "feminine mystique." At that time, he thought, with

19

those big amber eyes, thin legs and mane of taffy-colored hair, she had about as much feminine mystique as a spindly-legged palomino colt.

Peter tapped the bowl of his pipe to empty the ashes into an ashtray. Well, Hensley Travis had grown up a bit. He smiled. And quite attractively, at that. The last time he had seen her, a year ago at her father's funeral, there had been no sunglasses masking her pretty face. He remembered her eyes luminous with tears.

"Mr. Merrick . . ." Emma's voice claimed his attention. "I talked with John Martin. He's on his way over now to meet with you."

"Oh, that's good. Thank you, Emma." Peter lifted the large piece of copper ore that was mounted on an ebony base and served as a paperweight, and pulled out several sheets of paper. With the environmental-control report in front of him, he got busy with his work for the day.

Chapter 3

Allan gripped the steering wheel as he caught sight of the mountains. Had they always looked so rugged? Or was it that now, for the first time in his thirty-two years, he desperately needed their symbol of strength? The highest peak, he noticed, wore a mantle of snow as a priest wears his white surplice. He frowned at the thought.

His gaunt shoulders ached with weariness. Maybe he should have taken Peter's advice, made the trip by plane, but he had felt a compulsive need to drive once again along these familiar roads. He remembered other springtimes here in Montana. Then, as now, winter was beginning to relinquish her snow-white hold to the April sun.

Rotating his head to stretch the muscles of his neck, he consciously relaxed his shoulders and turned his attention again to driving. The wide highway rolled smoothly ahead. He found himself wishing the traffic were heavier; he would welcome distraction from the thoughts that plagued his mind.

Should he have come to burden Peter with his schemes? A week ago it seemed the only course left open to him. Involuntarily his fingers tightened around the wheel. He swore silently at the sight of the blue veins so clearly visible beneath the thin skin on the back of his hands.

He was now less that fifteen miles outside Anaconda. Sighting his turnoff, Allan flicked the turn signal, eased his foot on the gas pedal and swung the car smoothly to the right onto the wide ribbon of black top that wound along the sloping terrain. He pursed his lips in a whistle of a sigh. Thank God, he was almost there.

At the crest of a slightly rising hill he saw the familiar panoramic view of Peter's ranch spreading out before him. It was a diamond-shaped area of land with the house set back a few hundred yards from the forward point of the diamond. The beauty of the Merrick land lay in the low rolling hills beyond the house. Between these tree-covered hills lay valleys of deep grass and one narrow streambed along the sides of which grew the bitterroot that in another few weeks would bear pink and white blossoms. Allan smiled, for he knew that tomorrow he and Peter would ride two of the mares along this stream.

As he drove through the gate he noticed that the fence enclosing the ranch showed patches of new wire which glistened now in the slender rays of the late-afternoon sun. He smiled. How characteristic this was of Peter's competent handling of all that belonged to him. He would make certain that new wire was stretched to replace a broken area the very day it was discovered, just as a downed fence post would be immediately righted and firmly replanted on any section of Merrick property.

Now approaching the house, Allan welcomed the sight of those rust-colored brick walls and the weathered gray shingles of the low-eaved roof. Pulling into the driveway, he had scarcely switched off the ignition before the front door swung open and Peter, with several of those long strides of his, was at Allan's side.

"You made good time; I knew you would!" Peter said, clapping Allan's shoulders in hearty welcome. "God, it's great to have you here!" He reached in the backseat for the luggage.

Peter had ducked his head quickly, but not before Allan caught the flash of pain that marked his face. Allan realized his appearance would be a shock to his friend, for he had dropped twenty pounds since the last time the two of them had been together.

"Am I ever glad to be here too, Pete! You and Georgie Girl are a sight for sore eyes," he said as the black-and-tan mixed-breed terrier nuzzled his hand, asking to have her neck ruffled. Allan obliged, also rubbing the thick hair along her back. The dog shimmied her hips and wagged her cropped tail in joyous greeting. The two men entered the house with the dog trotting so close to Allan's legs that she brushed against his trousers.

"Being here is just the tonic I need," Allan said, feeling the embrace of those familiar walls.

"We can take this up later." Peter set Allan's two-suiter by the newel post.

Allan let his gaze follow the wide steps of the mahogany staircase as it rose gracefully from the entrance hall to the landing halfway up and then curved to complete its climb to the second floor. The color of the wood had the same mellow tone as the burnished copper lantern that hung from the high ceiling of the entry hall.

"I'll fix us both a drink," Peter said, heading for the kitchen.

Allan nodded and walked on ahead into the living room. Thank God nothing changes here, he thought, noting the gray-blue of the walls that appeared to fuse into the matching draperies at the windows. The cool blue of the room was warmed by the deep red Oriental rug that covered a large portion of the polished wood floors. He settled his lean body into a comfortable position on the sofa and let scenes of the Thanksgiving and other holiday weekends he had spent here sift pleasantly through his mind.

Peter returned, handing him a tall glass of Scotch and water. Georgie Girl followed her master and took her place in front of the hearth. She chose her spot very precisely; lying down, she positioned her head on her front paws so as to observe both of them with her shiny brown eyes.

"How peaceful this room is. I envy you this beautiful old house, Pete. Sure beats hell out of that glass-and-concrete place I live in."

"Yeah," Peter agreed. "I'm glad Dad held on to it. When Mother died, he thought of selling the place. He didn't see much point in keeping it, with her gone. You know, she was the one who loved the horses and the land. Well . . . Dad never came up with a buyer, and I'm glad." Peter leaned back in the wine-red chair next to the sofa and placed his feet on the ottoman.

"I can't imagine anyone else here in this house but you. Can you?" Allan asked, twirling the ice slowly in his glass.

"No, of course I can't. I've lived my entire life right

here. When the right girl comes along, who knows, maybe I'll settle down and another family of Merricks can grow up on the ranch."

"I'll drink to that." Allan lifted his glass. "Here's to the Merrick dynasty!"

Peter laughed. "Before the 'dynasty,' there's going to have to be a complete fresh paint job on the inside of this house. Matter of fact, I'm having some redecorating done in here starting next month."

"I'm glad I'm seeing the old paint job." Allan paused and eyed the room again. "I'm afraid I hate to see anything change anymore. I simply want everything to stay exactly as it is—as long as it possibly can!" He could feel Peter's eyes watching him. Silence followed his words. Peter kept looking at him. Allan saw the anxiety revealed in his friend's face.

"How are things really going for you?" Peter asked finally.

Turning his hand from side to side, his gesture foreshadowed his words. "So-so." He shrugged. "As they say, there's good news and bad news." He rubbed his hand absently over the arm of the sofa. "The good news is that I've really felt pretty well since I had blood transfusions in December. I get tired, there's no denying that, but in lots of ways these past four months have been great. In fact, some of the best," he added, smiling. "You see, there is this girl!"

"You can't be too tired if you found energy to cultivate a new girl!" Peter gave Allan a tongue-in-cheek grin.

"Not just *a* girl." Allan grinned back.

"You underscore it like it should read *the* girl," Peter challenged. "Are you telling me you drove all the way to Montana to ask me to be best man at a wedding?" Peter boomed out, his dark blue eyes bright with pleasure at such a thought.

"God knows, I'd give anything to be able to say that

24

was the reason for my trip! The way things are now . . ." He shook his head. "I'm afraid it's damn unlikely!" Draining his glass, he set it down on the coffee table in front of him. "Two weeks ago, I would have said it was a certainty, but now . . ." He put his face in his hands, rubbing his temples. "I made a mistake with Karen. I should have told her when I first met her in October about the leukemia, but I didn't. Truth is, I only told her a few days before I made this trip."

"Why did you wait so long?"

"Well, now, that's a good question. One I've analyzed for myself at least a hundred times. Possibly, if I explain it all to you, Pete, you can give me a different perspective."

"Try me," Peter responded quietly.

Shifting his position, Allan stretched his legs, crossing his feet. This is what I need, he thought. Getting feedback from Peter would straighten out his thinking just as it had countless times in the past. He smiled to himself, knowing it had always been that way for the two of them. "Her name is Karen Blake," he began, keeping his tone easy. "She's a secretary for a legal firm in Duluth. One that handles many of our company's shipping contracts for the Mesabi ore area. We met the first of October, and . . . well, everything seemed right for both of us from the start. So, I found every possible reason in the book to be in Duluth from then on!" He cocked his head. "You wouldn't believe how good-looking she is!"

"I believe it—I assure you, I believe it!" Peter countered with mock seriousness. "At any rate, I know better than to argue with you. If memory serves me, I've always agreed with your evaluation of feminine beauty since our freshman days, when you charmed that redheaded cheerleader away from me! You do recall that episode, don't you? That was a dirty trick,

25

ol' miner!" He shook his fist at Allan. "You may not know it, but it took me a while to forgive you for that one." His mouth spread into a grin.

"Hell, Pete! I had almost forgotten about her. She was really stacked." He began to laugh. "I do remember that!"

"Let's forget the rah-rah girl and get back to your Karen. Tell me, what does Hensley think about her?"

"Truth is, Hensley's never met Karen. I had planned on getting them together at Christmas—then I got sick again." He frowned. "That's when I went into the hospital for transfusions." Glancing over at Georgie Girl, who was noisily licking her paws, he watched her for a minute, then continued. "I should have leveled with Karen about my condition right then, but dammit!—everything was so perfect between us. I was afraid, I guess. I didn't want to rock the boat. Can you understand?"

Peter nodded.

"I lied to her. Said I had to go in the hospital for a few simple tests. Said I'd lost weight—might be, I was anemic." He could feel tension building inside him. "I loved her—I didn't want to risk losing her—I couldn't handle it." He had made tight fists of his hands as he spoke. Straightening his cramped fingers, he rubbed his palms together.

"I don't think you have a major problem there, if she loves you," Peter said. "You're feeling fine since those transfusions, you said so yourself. You're in remission. I'd say you and Karen have a future together!"

Allan shook his head slowly. Without answering, he got up and turned his back to Peter. Walking across to the windows, he stood, holding his back rigid and looking out for several silent moments before he finally spoke. "No," he said without turning around. "I'm not in remission."

Peter sucked in his breath. The dog jerked awake, alerted by the harsh sound.

"I thought I was—prayed I was. My lab tests just ten days ago were conclusive. There is no hope of remission now." Turning, he looked over at Peter. "That's why I called last week. Why I insisted on coming at this time. As to Karen, and our relationship . . ." He shrugged. "The decision is hers. Chances are, she's already decided to end things between us." He took a few steps away from the window. "What's important now concerns Hensley. It's imperative I make financial arrangements to ensure her security. I need your help, Peter, to do this. I have to know she will be provided for when I'm gone."

"My God, Allan!" Peter bolted from his chair. "Don't talk like that! You're alive—hell, man, you're going to stay alive!" Peter held Allan's shoulders in a fierce grip. "There's time—you've got lots of time yet!"

"No, I don't. What I have is possibly three months, maybe less." The sound of his own voice surprised him. He had managed the words in an even and completely detached tone. He wondered if he could continue to mask his inner turmoil by a display of outward calm.

"Look, it's O.K. At least, Pete, it will be O.K. if you wipe that damn look off your face!" He gave him a couple of fast punches in the shoulder, hoping to lessen the tension between them. "I've driven way out west for your help, old buddy. .What I need from you is not your sympathy, but your strength!"

"You've got it!" Peter's jaw set firmly. "Whatever— whenever—you've got it!"

Allan's mouth twisted in a half-smile. "I've faced up to the facts, but I haven't accepted them all with the best grace. What really bugs me is, I'm not leaving anything of myself behind. Maybe I'm an egotist," he said, jabbing his hands in his pockets. "But God knows, I hate to have nothing to show for my thirty-two years. I'd like to leave my mark on something!" Averting his eyes from the concerned expression on

27

Peter's face, he walked over and picked up his empty glass. "Before I get too maudlin, you'd better freshen my drink."

Allan welcomed the few minutes alone. He sank wearily into Peter's chair; it felt good to put his feet up. He thought he had never been quite this tired before. He closed his eyes briefly. The blackness of his eyelids seemed strangely peaceful. He thought again of the drive out, seeing the mountains and the way their snowcapped peaks pierced the low-floating clouds this morning. He knew he had done the right thing in coming.

Returning, Peter handed a fresh drink to Allan. "Let's talk about Hensley. Let me hear the plans you have for her."

Allan clicked his glass against Peter's. He realized the effort Peter was making to keep the conversation between them unemotional. "Here's to my sister! You and I are going to see to it that she can scale any mountain she chooses," Allan stated loudly. "We accomplish that, and I'll be satisfied!"

"O.K. Let's tackle the problem, then." They lifted their glasses and drank to each other.

"Hensley's inheritance is no large fortune, but there will be enough to cushion life for her." Allan smiled, adding, "With careful management, that is. That's where you come in, my friend!"

"Wise management—you came to the right man," Peter boasted.

"Don't brag too soon. You'll have the impetuous Miss Travis to contend with as well as her finances. It won't be an easy job." Allan chuckled. "She's young, you know. Younger, in some ways, than her twenty-two years. At least she seems that way to me." He narrowed his eyes thoughtfully. "Dad and I both over protected her, I suppose. We're to blame if she's a mite spoiled." He grinned broadly. "And a mite spoiled she is!"

"Well, overprotected and spoiled isn't fatal. She may surprise us when she's on her own."

"I wish I could count on it." He paused, taking a swallow of Scotch. "Dad indulged her—wanting to make it up to her somehow for her losing Mother. Hensley was only ten when Mother was killed in a car accident, you know. At any rate, Hensley is often extravagant, and also she does get carried away by some of her whims and causes." Allan shook his head, feigning long-suffering tolerance of his sister's behavior. "I figure a trust is the sensible financial arrangement," he said, taking another swallow of his drink. "With you acting as trustee, Pete, I'd know you could hold a firm rein on her. Hensley is great"—he grinned—"truly she is, but it's only fair to warn you, she'll give you a few headaches."

"I can handle that," Peter said. "At least"—he raised one eyebrow—"I think I can."

"Beyond the financial aspects, I'm apprehensive about her, because she'll be completely alone. I'm all the family she has—not even the proverbial maiden aunt. What I'm really getting at . . ." He eyed Peter solemnly. "I want you to take care of her—literally!"

"You what?" Peter's voice rose in bewilderment. "What are you laying on me here?" He crossed his arms. "Look here, Allan! Hensley is of legal age, and that's a bit old for a guardian. Anyway," he went on, "how can I look after her if she's in Minnesota and I'm in Montana?"

"Right on! You've got it!" Allan leaned forward, shaking his finger in Peter's face.

"Hold on, there." Peter shook his head. "That look on your face scares me! You have the exact expression I remember from college, when you were about to talk me into one of your fantastic schemes. As I so well recall, in all of those the outcome was disaster for me, but you, friend, came off scot-free!"

Allan brushed off Peter's words with a wave of his

hand. "This is no wild scheme, I swear it isn't. You and I can work out a plan of action. We can figure out just the right way to maneuver Hensley. We'll simply get her out here to Montana some way. Then you can keep an eye on her."

"Whoa, now! Put a bridle on some of that enthusiasm. You're putting out a big order there."

"You can pull it off, Peter. If anyone can handle Hensley, you can." He grinned. "I've got a feeling about this, and I know you can make it work." He drew several quick breaths. He realized his excitement had literally taken his breath away. He allowed his shoulders to sag, indulging for a moment in hating his energyless body.

"I appreciate your confidence, but you know, don't you, that your sister may take a very dim view of any plans you and I make for her? My experience with the opposite sex has shown me they resent being told what to do!" A knowing smile curved his mouth.

"We won't tell her," Allan said, rubbing his hand across his forehead. "At least, not any more than we have to."

"It might be possible, at that. I could offer Hensley a job at the company. It could just work." He concentrated his gaze on his friend's face. "I'll give it the old college try, for your sake." His words were light, but Allan knew there was concerned purpose in Peter's statement.

"I knew I could count on you, Pete!" He stood up. He felt better. He even felt a little bit of strength move through him. "With your help, all will be right for Hensley—and that makes it right for me." He put his hand on Peter's shoulder. "Thanks! God knows, I'm grateful to you!" He let his breath out, still holding a firm grip on Peter's shoulder. "Hell, Pete, finish that drink of yours and go get some steaks on the grill. This mountain air of yours has given me the biggest appetite I've had in six months!"

Chapter 4

Hensley decided not to write Allan about her job, but to wait and surprise him with her news when he came for her graduation. She wanted to be able to see his reaction. When she did tell him, her brother's look of total astonishment fed her ego.

"Ha-ha! You can't believe I did it all by myself, can you?" she said, focusing her eyes on his face and reveling in the little drama she was creating.

"I'm amazed! I admit it." He frowned slightly.

"Great, isn't it?"

"Yeah—great—of course it is." Although he moved his mouth into a smile, Hensley sensed he was less than enthusiastic.

"Well, I must say, you could rave a bit and give out with the I'm-so-proud-of-my-smart-little-sis routine," she prodded him.

"Hey, I'm proud of you all right," he said, raising his hand in a mock salute. "I'm just surprised. You must admit it's a bit unexpected. I guess I didn't realize what a budding journalist there was in the family." He smiled. "I should have known you would tackle job hunting with the same eager-beaver impulsiveness you apply to everything else you do." He paused, and glancing at his watch, began to pull at the expandable band, adjusting it to a lower position on his wrist.

"It's rather an odd coincidence," he continued, "but while I was at Peter's, he inquired about your plans following graduation. He had in mind offering you a job with the Merrick Copper Company."

31

"That's foolish! Why on earth would I go out to Montana to work?" She tossed her hair back and shrugged at such an absurd idea. "Allan, you know very well I wouldn't leave Ironville, with you here!"

Seeing the stricken expression that marked Allan's gaunt face, she pressed her lips together, shutting off her words. In the sudden hammering silence, realization pounded down upon her. Of course she would not leave Ironville, with her brother here. *Never as long as he was here.* But how long might that be? Fingers of fear pressed against her windpipe. She swallowed, unable to speak. She could not bear the anguish revealed in her brother's eyes. She turned her head away.

After graduation, the warm days of June arrived. Attacking her new job with zeal, Hensley found work at the Ironville *Daily Journal* to her liking. David Gillette worked closely with the staff, making for a camaraderie which manifested itself in the newspaper's success. She soon discovered David's outspoken honesty was definitely "on target." You were never in doubt as to where you stood with the editor of the *Journal.*

"Hensley, hiring you is turning out to be wise as well as expedient," he said to her at the end of her third week on the job. "Equal opportunity for women is so damn big these days, even here in conservative old Ironville. I actually let you talk me into employing you to give the paper the progressive image of a better proportion of women to men on our payroll." He raised one eyebrow. "I'm a *hell* of a smart man at that!" The way he was tossing his red head made Hensley think of an arrogant rooster. David grinned at her. "I got a willing worker with a fair share of ability in the bargain." He pulled off his glasses, peering at her in amusement. Then, waving his glasses like a clock pendulum, he added, "I just may be able to make a first-rate newspaperman out of you—strike that—newspaper *person* I intended to say!" He walked away from her desk in laughter.

She knew this was his way of showing his approval of her, and it made her feel good. From her first encounter with David Gillette, she had speculated about him. She had picked up a few details about his home life from casual office talk. Only yesterday she had heard David's wife was leaving the first of July to spend two months at some expensive lake resort in northern Minnesota. The rumors were rampant that the Gillette marriage was stormy, and David made no secret of his wife's extravagant habits.

"That wife of mine thinks I print money on these presses instead of a daily paper," he had said once in Hensley's presence. "God knows, she even spends it as if there will be another edition tomorrow!"

Hensley wondered if she listened to this gossip about David and his wife merely to help crowd the destructive thoughts of Allan's deteriorating condition from her mind. She tried, at all times now, to hide her concern from him, for she was determined to make this summer as easy for him as she possibly could.

Each evening after dinner she and her brother would sit and talk together on the patio. The June night air was laden with the scent of honeysuckle. She loved the fragrance. Thank goodness, she thought, the ultramodern aspects of the apartment complex made this concession to the otherwise evergreen landscaping. Along the concrete-block walls that outlined the parking area meadowsweet and honeysuckle had been planted. Tonight the perfume of the blossoms was so profuse it seemed to taste like honey on her tongue.

"Where do you want to sit?" Allan asked, coming through the sliding glass doors from the living room. He put the iced tea he was carrying on the metal table by the glider and turned to slide the doors closed. "Don't want to let any June bugs in the apartment."

33

"Or mosquitoes," Hensley added. "Let's sit together here on the glider, Allan. Then I can hear you when your noisy neighbor turns up the volume on his TV." She brushed her words with a laugh, but she was quite serious about wanting to hear all of his words. These nightly conversations had an important immediacy about them, and she sensed it was vital to her brother to tell her all the things on his mind. The mild summer nights, the fragrant air, the umbrella of stars overhead, formed a setting in which Allan seemed to relax and reminisce. She felt happy listening as he pulled happenings from the depths of his memory and held them out to her. The bits of family memorabilia which were the keepsakes of his thirty-two years, he offered now to her like a gift. The wonderful aspect of these conversations was that he did not allow his words to be marred by sadness.

"Hensley, I wish you knew more about Dad's stamp collection," he said, leaning back against the green glider cushions. "When you have time, maybe you'll study some of them. They're interesting, you know. Some are quite beautiful. Like lots of hobbies, stamp collecting can get in your blood."

"I've become aware of that fact just lately," she said, pulling off her shoes and tucking her feet under her legs Indian fashion. "I'd even go so far as to say with some people stamps can be an obsession."

"How's that?" She could see she had aroused his interest.

"My boss, David Gillette, acts like an avid collector. Why, he even asked me about buying a pair of Dad's Canadian stamps. He's really interested."

"*No Sale!*" Allan thrust out his hand in a halt signal. "I certainly would not break up that Canadian series! And I hope you'll want to keep the collection intact," he added, reaching for his glass of tea. "That is, of course, unless you really need to sell for an emergency.

Be sure it's really necessary before you dispose of any stamps, because Dad felt they would offer a measure of security for us."

Allan's tone was deadly serious. She smiled to reassure him. "Don't worry." She shook her head to emphasize what she was saying. "I promise, I won't throw away my legacy."

"I know you won't. It will be yours, however, and you may use it any way you like. There's not a fortune there, but the series would bring about fifty thousand dollars." He put his hand on hers. "Sell any or all, if it should be that important to you. I would—for a great enough cause!"

He stood up, putting his hand in his pants pocket. "The stamps are in my safe-deposit box. Now, I've already had you sign a card giving you authorization to enter the box. Here, I want to give you a key." As he spoke, he pulled his key case from his pocket, and removing one, handed it to her.

Hensley's fingers trembled as she closed them over the flat, rather uninteresting-looking key. It felt slick. It slipped between her fingers; for an instant she fumbled, almost dropping it. The absurd thought passed through her mind that this was a very ugly small key without any grace of design or proportion. She found she had clenched her teeth as she tried to rid herself of this idea. She was stubbornly determined to pass over this bit of action of Allan's. She rebelled against it, for there was a hopeless finality in his giving her the deposit-box key. She closed her eyes against the ugly blot this incident had made on the mosaic of their June evenings.

After she went to bed, she lay quietly, waiting for sleep to come. Unbidden, thoughts of the key Allan had given her returned, and her process of thought association brought another one to mind. The brass door key to the apartment—the one the dark-haired girl had used and left behind. She had almost forgotten that April afternoon. Could she ask Allan about it? Who the girl had been? What had happened to her? What would be the good of mentioning it to him now? The girl who had come looking for him probably had not come back. After all, she had been crying when she ran away—and too, she had left the key behind.

Mid-July this year brought days that were unusually hot for Minnesota. Coming in from the outside heat, Hensley felt the sharp coolness of the hospital corridor prickle the flesh of her bare arms. It was more than the air conditioning. In these nine days since her brother entered the hospital, the chill of apprehensive fear had begun to envelop all her senses.

Allan was hanging up the telephone as she entered his room. She had been in such a hurry to get here, and now she could not help but wish she had been delayed. She might then have escaped the pain of the scene that greeted her. There was a look of naked agony on her brother's ashen face, the sight of which brought tears to her eyes.

Moving quickly to his bedside, she lifted one of his thin hands and held it firmly between her tanned ones. She said nothing. For some inexplicable reason she felt reticent. Perhaps the truth was that she wanted to avoid knowledge of anything that could affect Allan so painfully. His hand felt cold. She could see the ridges of blue veins through his transparent skin.

Sitting on the bed, she hesitantly began to talk of inconsequentials, the unusual heat, the possibility of rain, even the copy she had been writing this afternoon for the paper. If he listened, he gave no overt sign. Hensley sensed his thoughts were far away from this hospital room.

Walking to the window, she examined a brass container planted with variegated greenery. It appeared to be a new addition to the flowering plants that decorated the marble windowsill. Picking up the florist card, she asked, "Who's Karen?" She placed an inflection of teasing inquisitiveness to the question in an effort to lighten the mood which still pervaded the room.

Thinking he had not heard, when he failed to answer, she spoke again. "Allan, who's this Karen that sent this pretty planter? Have you been keeping secrets from your sister?" she prodded with a laugh.

"Maybe I have," he finally answered in a low voice. "She's a girl I know."

"Special girl?"

"Very special to me."

She waited for him to elaborate, but he did not comment further. A dozen questions needled her tongue. Who was this Karen? Where was she? If she were indeed special to Allan, why, then, didn't his own sister know her? When did this special Karen visit Allan? Odd she had never run into her here at the hospital. So many whos and whys pushed against her lips. She closed her mouth firmly on all these questions, almost afraid to ask any one of them. She kept still, waiting for Allan to say something more. Realizing that he evidently was not going to explain, she said gently. "I've never—ever—heard you mention a Karen."

Allan shifted his shoulders, raising himself into a sitting position. She could hear his labored breathing. Even lifting his head higher on the pillows seemed an obvious effort for him tonight.

"I planned once, some months ago, to talk to you about Karen, but I told Peter instead. I've always found it easier to talk with Peter than with anyone else," he said thoughtfully. He ran his hand through his light hair, then placed both hands beneath his head, a position he often assumed when settling into a conversation. Hensley found this suddenly reassuring.

"I started going with Karen before I was really ill and

while there was still hope for remission. After that—well—there didn't seem much point in talking about a love affair that had no future.''

She stared at him as if searching his face for the pieces of the puzzle that were still missing. "Maybe you'd rather I didn't ask," she said shyly, "but why did it end abruptly?"

"Because I learned I had no future to offer her. No healthy one, that is. She didn't want to continue a relationship with a dying man." Bitterness edged his words.

Hensley's hand tensed, and the florist's card slipped from her fingers. As she bent over to retrieve it, the neat letters written across the paper blurred. Instead of black words on white paper, she saw the image of a flawless face framed by ink-black hair. Still staring at the card, she said, "If Karen is a petite brunette with green eyes, then I met her once."

"You've met Karen?" Allan gaped at her in disbelief. "When? Where?" His voice rang out in the room with revitalized vigor. "Why didn't you tell me before?"

"I wanted to, and maybe I should have. Heaven knows, I was plenty curious, but I didn't want you to think I was being the nosy little sister prying into your affairs." She laid the card beside the plant and walked to Allan's bed. "You never bombarded me with questions about the fellows I knew." She smiled. "I figured your romances were your own business."

"Don't kid around, please. I want to know everything about you and Karen. It's important!" He had pushed himself upright in the bed and was looking intently at her.

"It was the weekend in April when I drove down from school to see about my job," she said, pulling a chair close to his bed. "You had gone to Montana to see Peter, but I didn't know that, of course. Karen came to the apartment looking for you." Hensley launched into the details of that afternoon, attempting to recall it as exactly as she could. Allan listened closely, a touch of color tinting his thin face. His blue eyes were bright with interest, and she thought they seemed to have regained their deep color for the first time in weeks.

She paused, wondering whether to mention the apartment key. She decided against it. "When she ran from the apartment so quickly," Hensley said instead, "I hadn't had time to find out her name or really anything about her. Only that she was looking for you. It was strange and awkward for both of us, Allan, not knowing where you were or when you would return."

"I can imagine." Allan nodded. "It's my fault, actually. You see, I kept it from Karen that I had leukemia. Then in April when my tests ruled out all hope of remission, I was forced to tell her the truth." He sank back against the pillows, shoulders sagging and his arms limp at his sides like broken boughs against a tree trunk. "When I did tell Karen, she took it badly. Wouldn't see or even talk to me." He frowned, and all the brightness had faded from his eyes. "The following week, I left and went out to Peter's."

"My God! She's cold as a snake! How could you care for a girl who'd walk out on you because you were sick?" Her voice rose in anger. "I hate *her!*"

"You don't understand, Hensley. You're so different from Karen! You're outgoing and you have a youthful courage." He reached out for her hand. "A *gutsy* gal, that's my sis!" He patted her hand, then took his away. "Karen's not like you—not like you at all." She could see his chest heave in a sigh. Turning his head slightly, he looked away from her face. "Did you know, Hensley," he said quietly, "there are some people who are so frightened of cancer, they're unable even to start to cope with the knowledge that someone they love has a malignancy—much less is dying from it. Karen is like that. She could not do what you did tonight—walk into this hospital room, take my hand, touch my face."

She covered her mouth with her hand, pressing hard

against her lips. So strong was her empathy for her brother, she felt sick with the knowledge of the suffering Karen had caused him. She knew she bore a deep, lasting malice toward this girl.

Abruptly she pushed her chair away from Allan's bedside. "You're tired," she said gently. "We shouldn't have talked about this." Turning, she gathered up the evening paper, laid it on top of some magazines and nervously fingered the items on the table by the bed, arranging things in order. She deliberately kept from looking at her brother.

"Please, Hensley, stop fussing with those things and sit down here for a few more minutes. There's something else I must explain to you about Karen and me. You see, I did see her a little over two weeks ago. You remember, when I went to Duluth for the Fourth of July weekend. We were able to reach some important decisions." He paused. "I think I helped her."

Hensley stood leaning against the chair, her hands gripping the vinyl-covered back. "You helped *her!*" She lashed out in anger. "Why doesn't she help you? Dammit, she could evidence some concern—do something more considerate than send a potted plant." She slapped the chair. "And must she torture you with phone calls? That was Karen on the phone tonight—I know it had to be." She shook her head sadly. "Oh, Allan . . ." Hensley began to cry. "You looked so terrible when I came in." She moved to him, lifted his hand and held it to her cheek. "I can't stand to see you so sad!" She heard the quick intake of his breath.

"Look, I'm not sad. See, I'm even smiling." His colorless lips parted in a smile line. "But you're right, I am tired. We'll wait and talk about this tomorrow." He took his hand away and rubbed it on the sheet to wipe away her tears. "Promise me you won't think badly of Karen," he added. "I would like it if you two were friends."

She stared at him in silence, not wanting to answer.

Fortunately, the nurse came in at this moment with his medication. Hensley touched her brother's shoulder in good-bye and left the hospital.

Before dawn of the following day, Allan slipped into a coma. The remainder of the week became for Hensley a nightmare of silence and waiting. The impersonal kindness of the nurses angered her. The antiseptic odor of the hospital halls now filled her with a loathsome nausea. Her spirits warred against everything and everybody who seemed destined to separate her from her brother. Through these hours she recalled many times what Allan had said to her. "You're different from Karen. You have courage, Hensley. You're my gutsy little sis." *Gutsy*—it had a determined, bold ring to it. And Allan had always been right about things. He must be right about her, too.

Four days later, at four-thirty in the afternoon, she received a call from Dr. Bronson. It took her less than fifteen minutes to get from the newspaper office to the hospital. The doctor was standing outside Allan's room as she approached. He walked forward to meet her, his face grave. She knew without his saying a word that her brother was dead.

Later that evening, alone in the apartment, Hensley called Peter Merrick. When his voice came on the line, she found it difficult to speak. Her tongue seemed immobile in her dry mouth. Until this moment, she had not realized how unbelievably painful it would be for her to tell Peter that—Allan was dead.

"Peter . . ." Her voice broke. "Peter . . . oh, Peter . . ." she sobbed.

"Hensley! Oh, my God! Hensley, he's gone, isn't he?"

She could not answer. She kept nodding her head, as if Peter could see her across the miles.

"Are you all right?"

"Yes," she whispered.

"I'll be on the next plane. Don't worry—I'll be there to help you. Wait, and I'll take care of the arrangements." He paused. She heard him clear his throat. "I'll be there tomorrow. You get someone in to stay with you tonight—don't be alone."

"Yes, I will, Peter . . . and I'm fine, really I am. Peter, thank you, thank you for coming," she repeated, trying not to cry. "I didn't know who else to turn to, and Allan—he told me to call on you whenever—"

"Of course, Hensley—of course. That's right! I'll get there just as soon as I can. And I'm sorry . . . *God, I'm sorry!*"

She hung up the phone, keeping her hand tightly pressed to the black receiver as if it could offer her reassurance. Peter would handle everything, she thought. She knew she could count on him.

Involuntarily her body jerked at the sound of the doorbell. She wiped her face with a handkerchief as she went to the door.

David Gillette stood in the doorway. "I'm sorry about your brother," he said, putting his arms around her with an awkward gentleness. "Let me help you, Hensley. I want to do anything I can." Without pausing for her to acknowledge his words, he kept talking, his manner almost brusque in his obvious concern for her. "I bet you haven't eaten a bite since lunch. Come on, I'm going to get you some dinner."

She shook her head. "I'm not hungry, David, really."

"Of course you are! Furthermore, it will do you good to eat." He patted her shoulder. "I know a place just a few blocks from here. We can get a good steak."

She walked away from him, crossing the living room. With a sigh she pushed the long strands of her hair back from her face. "I can't." Reaching for the back of the sofa, she leaned against it for support. She felt drained, empty. "Thank you, anyway, but I don't want to see

42

any people tonight." She shook her head. "Besides, I'm too tired to do anything."

"This is a small restaurant. There won't be anyone there at this hour on a week night. Come on! I'll see we get a table in a corner." He came to her, rubbed his hand along her arm. "You have to eat, honey," he said softly. "It'll do you good."

What was the use of arguing? she thought. She didn't have the strength to resist. After all, David did want to be helpful. She shrugged. It was much easier to simply let him take over. "Give me a few minutes to fix my face," she said.

In her bedroom, she picked up a lipstick and pressed the coral color against her lips. Why am I letting David talk me into things? she questioned her image in the mirror. I lean, she thought. I leaned on Dad and then on Allan. They both seemed to want it that way, and I must have too. But now it's different. I'm not at all sure I want to lean on David Gillette—and I must not even start to depend on him!

She replaced the cap on the lipstick, touched her cheeks with a blusher to erase the look of fatigue, and brushed back her hair. Picking up her purse, she rejoined David. With a sigh of resignation she smiled at him. "You're right, I am hungry," she said.

He put his arm around her shoulders and they walked together out of the apartment. David's arm felt comforting to her. She leaned against him, ever so slightly.

The following morning, Peter called Hensley from Duluth. He had a short layover to change planes for the brief flight into Ironville. Hensley arrived at the small airport a few minutes before his flight was due. She waited behind the chain-link fence that bordered the runway. It was another warm morning, so she was glad she had dressed in a sundress and barefoot sandals. The noon sun poured down on the blacktop surface of the air strip and the wind felt hot blowing across the expanse of unsheltered ground.

The airplane touched down and rolled smoothly with diminishing speed to a final stop only fifty feet from the fence where she waited. As soon as the blocks were wedged beneath the wheels and the portable steps rolled into position, the door of the plane opened. Peter appeared in the doorway and ducked his brown head to clear the opening. He straightened quickly, standing tall, his eyes searching the waiting area. Catching sight of Hensley, he raised his hand, waved and hurried down the steps. He had removed his suit coat and carried it flung over his arm.

For just a moment her gaze returned to the open doorway of the plane as if she expected to see another figure, a lean, blond man, follow directly behind Peter. Her conscious mind was acutely aware she was doing just that—looking for Peter's companion. In all the years of the past, she had never seen Peter Merrick unless Allan had been there too. But this time—this July morning—Peter robustly alive and handsome walked toward her alone. Her brother was not there. He would never be there again. Hensley looked at Peter through her tears. Without either of them saying a word, the two people who had loved Allan so deeply put their arms around each other and clung together.

Church services for Allan were held the next afternoon, followed by a brief ceremony at the cemetery. Hensley, pale and quiet, stood at the graveside listening to the minister's final prayer. A canopy of white canvas protected the gathering from the afternoon sun, but the air was oppressively still. She held her tear-dampened handkerchief against her nose and mouth in an attempt to shut out the cloying scent of the funeral flowers.

David held her left arm, lending his support. He had

met her brother only once, so she was aware that his personal involvement was just his concern for her.

Peter, at her right, had his eyes on the pastor. Hensley could almost feel the rigid tension in his solemn stance. She remembered the happenings of yesterday. Peter had handled each detail with precision, aiding her with reassuring suggestions and relieving her of decisions she found too difficult to make.

Peter now lowered his head at the start of the prayer. She noticed he did not close his eyes, but appeared to stare at the grass at his feet. Hensley could see the pulsing at his temples, and how the clenched thrust of his jaw pulled his skin taut over his cheekbones. As the "Amen" was spoken, he took a step forward, extending his hand. She sucked in her breath as a tremor of ultimate sadness touched her. She knew Peter had thrust out his hand to halt the minister's words, to somehow prevent this placement of sacred finality on Allan's life.

The hushed group began to separate, moving silently across the green cemetery lawn. Some acknowledged Hensley with wordless nods, while others paused to touch her hand, offering brief words of sympathy.

"Are you ready to leave now?" David asked as the gathering dispersed.

She nodded and turned her head to look for Peter. She saw him a hundred yards away talking earnestly with a figure in a beige sleeveless dress. Though the face was shielded from view by Peter's wide shoulders, Hensley was acutely aware that the person was Karen Blake. She had glimpsed her earlier, standing at the edge of the gathering, her dark hair pulled back from her pale face, revealing those green eyes of hers marred by dark circles. The phrase "haunted by guilt" had come to Hensley's mind to describe the look of those eyes. She could not help but take some satisfaction in the thought. She wanted Karen to suffer for deserting

Allan! Because of the contempt she felt for this girl, she bristled with irritation seeing Peter involved in conversation with her.

"We'll walk on," she said, turning to David. "I know you need to check back at the newspaper, so please, do go. Peter will be with me in a minute." She sighed, attempting to smile as she said, "Thank you, David, for being here. I do appreciate all you've done."

He squeezed her hand. "I see Peter coming now, so I will go on." He paused, kissing her lightly. "I'll talk to you later," he said, and hurried toward the parking area.

"Hensley," Peter said, taking hold of her arm as he caught up with her. "That poor girl is ill with the burden of her sorrow for Allan." He gestured with his head in Karen's direction. "Turn around and wave to her, smile too if you will. I'll explain later." He stated his request in terse phrases, his eyes pleading with her.

He knows how I dislike Karen, she thought. Why is he asking me to do this? She narrowed her eyes in anger.

"Just nod to her, quickly please," he asked again. "Honest to God, Hensley, she's falling apart!"

Hensley glanced over her shoulder and moved her head in a curt bob. Peter's words echoed for a second in her mind, penetrating her barrier of animosity. Allan had loved this strange girl; he had asked her to be understanding, even friendly, toward her. Sobered by her thoughts, she raised her hand in a quick wave.

Karen lifted her hand in a return salute, holding her head high now in what appeared to be an attitude of relief.

"That was good of you," Peter said as they walked toward the car.

"I still don't understand. What was it all really about?" she asked, frowning.

"Karen was inquiring about a message. It seems she telephoned Allan one night last week to tell him she

46

would do whatever it was he had asked of her. She was unable to talk to him, because it was so late and he had already been given a sedative. The nurse, however, promised to deliver her message when he woke up."

He quickened his steps and went on talking. "I told her I'd ask you about it."

"I don't know if he ever got such a message. How could I?"

"The point is, you don't know that he didn't!"

"Honestly Peter!" She made no attempt to hide her exasperation. "Did you force me to indicate to Karen Blake that I knew her words reached my brother before he died!" She raised her voice in anger. "I think I know the night she meant, and if so, she had called him earlier and upset him terribly. So I'm glad she was unable to talk to him again and disturb him further!"

"That's the important thing. I believe she called back to make some kind of amends, to relieve his mind and possibly give him a bit of happiness."

She looked at him, speculating on his statements. She wondered, did Peter know more than he was telling her? She slowed her steps. She had been almost running to keep up with Peter's long strides. What did it matter anyway? she thought. She really did not care one way or the other about Karen. The only one she cared about was Allan—and Allan was gone.

Peter's face blurred as tears came again to her eyes. She must not cling to the sadness of this day. She must stop looking back, and look only ahead now. Shaking her head quickly, she hurried forward. She could see clearly—she was no longer crying.

Chapter 5

Hensley sat staring at the blank paper in her typewriter, her thoughts straying far afield from her afternoon's assignment. In the two weeks since Allan's death, it was becoming increasingly apparent to her that Peter Merrick was the only one who treated her as if she might be capable of organizing her own life. At least he was not as intent on restructuring her life pattern as David seemed to be. Though Peter had referred to the possibility of her moving to Montana and taking a job with his company, he had not belabored the idea. He had left Ironville with the casual promise to keep in touch.

She equated Peter with her brother; therefore it seemed natural to accept help from him. But David was an entirely different matter. How, she wondered, should she handle her relationship with the editor of the *Journal?*

The informal, first-name basis of the newspaper office seemed almost too casual and friendly. David, after all, was the boss as well as a married man twenty years her senior. Since her brother's funeral, he had engulfed her in concerned attention, asking her to have dinner with him every night. When she made an excuse, he ignored it. Finally, she even suggested that people seeing them together might misunderstand.

"My wife and I are separated, and every citizen of Ironville knows it," he had stated in his usual blunt manner. "She doesn't give a damn who I see, or, for that matter, what I do. What interests her is that I continue to pay her exorbitant bills, not a damn thing else!" He shrugged. "Furthermore, I hate eating alone! It's uninteresting, unappetizing, and gives me a bad case of indigestion." Making a wry face and tucking her arm though his, he had led her off to a Swedish restaurant for smörgasbord.

Hensley had ambivalent feelings about David. She was seeing too much of him and he was dominating her life. She must find ways to widen her circle of friends. She had better do it soon. She rolled the paper higher to allow for a wider heading. Positioning her fingers over the typewriter keys, she thought. What I need is to turn the dial, change the station, allow a new and different set of actors to fill the screen of my existence. Scooting her chair closer to her desk, she briskly typed in a lead sentence for her belated copy.

An hour and a half later, when she finished the story, she looked up to find David leaning over her desk. "Come on, turn that in and let's go someplace for dinner," he said.

"I'm sorry, David, not tonight. I'm beat and I have a dozen chores to do at the apartment." She managed a firm, irrevocable tone.

"Right, you should relax at your place. I'll pick up a couple of steaks and the makings of a salad and join you there." He took off his glasses and stuck them in his shirt pocket. "I'll cook and you can do whatever it is you need to do."

"No, David—no way!" She shook her head, but he was gone, heedless of her objections, as always. She chewed her lower lip, incensed by his steamroller tactics. He issues orders like an army sergeant, she thought. She swept pencils and paper clips into the drawer of her desk, slamming it shut in irritation.

Driving home, these aggravating thoughts continued to annoy her. Why, I'm like a puppet, she thought, manipulated with taut strings which make my every movement jerky, awkward. A sudden ridiculous notion struck her. If she were a puppet in a play, then the most auspicious thing that could happen would be for her strings to snap, allowing her to collapse at one corner of the stage, lie there unnoticed, no longer a participant in the scene.

Letting herself into the apartment, she tossed her purse and the mail she had just taken from the mailbox on the sofa. Crossing the living room, she slid open the glass door to the patio. Fingers of cool air touched her face; the feeling soothed her. Placing albums of country-rock on the stereo, she sat down on the sofa and picked up the mail. Noticing a letter from Peter, she opened it first.

Dear Hensley,

A brief letter to enclose your September trust check. I'm sending it early in case you are running short. This is the amount agreed on, but it can be adjusted, somewhat, to fit your needs, in case it does not prove adequate. Do let me know.

Can I tempt you to reconsider your decision about coming to Montana? My offer of a job still stands, of course, and though it would differ from your newspaper work, still it would involve some writing for trade publications. A competent journalist could enhance the image of Merrick Copper to a beneficial degree! I believe you would find this area of the copper industry interesting.

Remember, the mountains of Montana await you. Why not let them bring you the happiness and sense of belonging that they brought Allan?

Peter

She refolded the letter, rubbing the creased edges between her fingertips. "The mountains of Montana await you"—the phrase rolled gently in her mind. It held out a majestic serenity to her, which at this moment seemed both inviting and comforting. She was reminded of a time years ago when Allan had come home following his first year at the University of Montana.

"Bet you can't guess what the word 'Montana' means?" he had said to her.

"Who cares?" had been her flippant reply. As a saucy nine-year-old she cared nothing for semantics.

"Well, I'll tell you anyway," Allan had continued good-naturedly, ignoring her sassiness. "It is Spanish for 'mountain.' Out there they say Montana means mountain treasure. The treasure being the *oro y plata*—the gold and the silver. I should say the copper too." He laughed. "My roommate, Peter Merrick, would certainly insist that it means 'copper!' His father owns a copper company, so to Pete, that's the all-important ore."

She found herself smiling at these happy memories, her mood definitely improved.

She had just turned the stack of records to the flip side when David arrived, bursting into the apartment with even more than his usual joviality. He was holding a sack full of groceries in his right arm and had a long loaf of French bread tucked under his left arm, while at the same time holding a jug of wine in his left hand. It was obvious that he was pleased to the hilt with himself over his purchases. He extended the bottle of wine toward her, struggling awkwardly to prevent the loaf of bread from slipping from under his arm. The whole scene was a comic pantomime.

Hensley laughed in spite of herself. How could anyone be as exasperating as David had been earlier this afternoon, yet so disarmingly amusing as he appeared now? "Oh, David," she said. "You are beyond me! I surrender. There is just no way to cope with you, or indeed without you either." Throaty laughter rolled over her words.

Taking the wine, she led the way into the kitchen. "You have a week's ration here," she said, taking two varieties of lettuce, a carton of fresh tomatoes, cucumbers, radishes and a large bunch of green onions from the sack.

This was the prologue to the most enjoyable dinner they had shared in these past weeks. David broiled the steaks and sliced the crusty bread, while Hensley tossed salad greens with tangy herb dressing. David made a ceremony of pouring the burgundy wine, and the meal was enjoyed amidst a good deal of light talk and laughter.

As they lingered over after-dinner coffee, David dropped his bantering and began to speak very seriously.

"Hensley, I know I forced my way in here tonight, and I owe you an apology. The truth is, I wanted to tell you some things, and I preferred a quiet place where we would be alone."

His sudden seriousness and the scrutiny of his eyes made her a little uneasy. Cradling her coffeecup in her hands as she drank, she eyed him warily.

"You must know by this time that my wife and I find we are both happier living apart," he continued. "So we're getting a divorce." Hensley could not detect any rancor in his tone.

"I'm sorry . . . David, I am sorry to hear that."

"It's the only answer and it's best," he stated with finality. "I want you to know these last few weeks would have been deadly without you around." He leaned closer, and she heard the rough edge of emotion in his voice.

"It's been a lonely time for both of us, and perhaps we've helped each other."

The developing intimacy of their conversation made her uncomfortable. "Let me get you some more coffee," she said, rising quickly.

"No—no, I don't want any more. Just sit down so I can talk to you."

Attempting to ignore his request, she began clearing the table.

"Honey, won't you listen to me?" he said, following her into the kitchen. "You're acting as if you don't want to hear what I am very eager to tell you."

She was stacking plates on the kitchen counter. "In a minute, let me rinse these dishes," she said, trying to evade him.

David took hold of her arms and turned her around to face him. They stood close together, looking at each other. He moved his hands, caressing her arms. The pressure of his fingers communicated an emotional intensity that she hadn't expected. He put his mouth on hers, kissing her with a competent thoroughness. Sensations crescendoed within her that she found both exciting and frightening as well. For a fraction of time she envisioned herself again as a marionette manipulated by an artful master. She trembled in David's arms. He moved his lips from hers, and holding his face against her cheek, whispered words of endearment.

"Please, David . . . please . . ." Her voice sounded uneven, breathless.

"I want you, Hensley—I need you. I'll make you happy. Let me, darling!"

"You've surprised me, David." Tensing her shoulders, she pushed against his chest to ease from the closeness of his embrace. "I've surprised myself a little, too." She had a warm, heady feeling and wondered if she might be blushing.

"Don't tell me you didn't know where we were headed?" he said, not allowing her to move more than a step away from him. With his arm circling her waist, he led her into the living room and sat down beside her on the sofa.

Hensley quickly thrust her knees sideways, at the

same time edging her back into the corner of the sofa, thus placing a slight space barrier between David and herself. His last statement jackhammered her thoughts. Had she truly sensed just where their relationship might be heading? Had there been a growing awareness she had refused to admit to herself? The older men who had figured in her life before David had been her father and brother. They both offered protective devotion without placing any demands upon her. From that first afternoon at the *Journal* office, hadn't she placed David in the father role?

She lowered her eyes, wanting to shield her thoughts from David's perceptive gaze. He watched her closely, as if examining every nuance of expression that her face might disclose. Keeping her head bowed, she rubbed her fingers across her hairline, at the same time masking her face with her hand. She had a guilty feeling winding through her mind like serpentine ribbon, for she knew she had never actually discouraged his attentions. To the contrary, she had reveled a bit in the concern her boss had shown her these past weeks since her brother's death. If she had seen David as a father image, it was short-lived. She must admit she had responded to his personal magnetism. Now it appeared quite clear to her that his desires were placing demands upon her. She felt a warm flush spreading along her throat.

David ran his hand though his rusty hair, his blue eyes warm and smiling. Nudging her knees away so he could reach her, he pulled her close. As he eased her shoulders down into the cushions of the sofa, his kisses searched the hollow of her throat. She had a sudden desire to escape the touch of his experienced hands. Like a child in a game of blindman's buff, she wished to slip from his grasp, duck and run from this intimate contact.

Suddenly she blurted out words she did not realize

she was even considering. "I'm leaving Ironville! I'm going to Montana!" Once she'd voiced this, she raced ahead, pouring out explanations. "Allan felt I should take a job there in his friend's company. You know, Peter Merrick? You met him at the funeral. He has a copper company, I could work for him. It's some kind of trade writing. Allan thought this would be the best thing for me to do. I've decided—"

He laid his hand gently across her trembling mouth. "Stop it, Hensley! Stop talking. I get the picture. God knows, I don't mean to frighten you away from me. That's the farthest thing from my mind!" He stood up, pulling her to her feet beside him. "I should have waited until my divorce was behind me." He stood quietly looking into her face, searching her eyes as if they might reveal something more to him.

"Good night," he said finally, and walked toward the door. With his hand on the doorknob, he turned back and with a slight toss of his head flashed a smile. "You know, you're running scared, Hensley Travis!" His voice had that same strident quality she remembered from their first meeting. "But at least you feel strongly enough about me to have to run! I think you may discover you are more frightened of yourself and your own emotions than you are of mine," he said, his voice assuming a gentle quality unusual in him. He opened the door. "I plan to wait around to see!" He left, closing the door silently behind him.

She stared after him, a potpourri of emotions whirling through her. How long she remained standing there probing her mind for answers, she did not know. One logical thought emerged. She could not stay here and work at the *Journal*. "I do want to leave Ironville!" She said the words aloud as if she needed to convince herself.

She walked with determination to the telephone; lifting the receiver, she began to dial.

"Peter, how are you? This is Hensley."

"Why, Hensley, this is a surprise! Good to hear your voice."

"Your letter came today, and I . . . I want to thank you for sending the trust check. I . . . ." She stammered nervously. She felt unsure of her decision, now that she actually had Peter on the line.

"Do you need some more money? Is that why you called?"

"No . . . no, in fact, I'm solvent at the moment." She laced her words with a laugh. Peter sounded so friendly and helpful, she felt easier. "I called to tell you I've begun to realize you're right about my coming to Montana."

"What? Do you mean it?"

"Yes, I do. I . . . well, I find I don't want to stay in Ironville after all."

"You've taken me completely by surprise." He laughed. "I have to be honest and admit it!" His voice echoed his astonishment. "I hoped you would come, of course, and we both know Allan wanted it very much. That's why I've kept encouraging you to consider the move." There was a second of silence. "But when I was there in Ironville and you and I talked about it you sounded so certain that you wanted to stay and work for the newspaper."

She could tell by his tone, he really had believed she would never come. "Things have changed for me here." She hesitated. "I feel I should leave. In fact, it's best that I do."

"Fine—that's fine! I'm glad, Hensley. I'm very glad." His reiteration perturbed her.

"Why, Peter, you really didn't think I'd take you up on your offer, did you?" She attempted to laugh to cover her embarrassment. "Have I put you on the spot? Maybe you don't have a job available for me right now? Would it be better for you if I waited until later on?" She rushed her words, feeling inept.

"Not a chance! Listen to me, the job is waiting! It's yours, and the sooner the better. You know Allan would be so pleased with your decision. I assure you, I am too! You're doing the right thing, but . . ." He began to chuckle. "You're some kind of an enigma to me, you know that? I'll be damned if you're not." He was laughing now. "It's all settled, then. How soon can I expect you?"

"I'll finish out the month here and then drive out. I should be there by September third or fourth. And, Peter, thank you."

"You don't need to thank me, Hensley. You're a mighty welcome addition. I'm looking forward to having you here." He paused. "I am a bit curious about what caused you to change your mind, however." There was a questioning inflection in his voice.

She did not reply. She was still searching her own mind for the answers.

"Hensley? Are you still there?"

"Yes, but I was busy thinking about seeing those mountains you and Allan have touted so," she answered wistfully. "I hope they're as spectacular as I've been led to believe all these years."

"Come see for yourself," he countered.

As she hung up, she was thinking of Peter saying she was an enigma to him. Not only to him, but to herself as well, she thought. David had told her she was running scared. Was she? Tossing her head, she thought of Allan telling her she had courage and calling her gutsy. She found that reassuring. She wasn't running scared, she was shifting gears, moving ahead with independence. Wasn't that today's self-assertive way to put it? Squaring her shoulders, she pushed a smile to her lips. She had taken the first step. She would go where mountains wait. Who knows, she might find one exactly right for climbing.

Chapter 6

September was putting a golden haze over the Montana countryside; the trees were yellowing and the grass had already faded to a warm beige color. As she drove along this morning, Hensley noticed even the sky seemed yellow. She thought: This is the "yellow morning sky" the artist Charles Russell immortalized in his Western landscapes.

She had enjoyed the drive from Minnesota. Traffic had been light on the highways, and the towns she had passed through were, for the most part, quiet, relaxed villages. It appeared that the majority of the population of North Dakota and central Montana lived on wheat farms and cattle ranches. She had passed by herds of cattle and sheep feeding on the needle grass on either side of the asphalt roadway. For much of the trip she saw only vast expanses of land stretching out around her.

She had allowed herself three days to make the trip from Ironville to Anaconda, and she was well ahead of schedule. As her eyes traveled to the buttes that lined the horizon, she glanced at her wristwatch. She should easily reach her destination by noon.

Anaconda was a city of fewer than twelve thousand, and Hensley had no difficulty in locating the offices of the Merrick Copper Company. Hesitating in the doorway, she smiled uncertainly. "Is this Mr. Merrick's office?" she asked the pleasant-looking woman sitting behind a desk near the center of the room.

"Yes, it is. May I help you? Her deep-set dove-gray eyes looked inquiringly at Hensley.

"I'd like to see him, if I may. I'm Hensley Travis."

"Of course; I'm Emma Carlson." The woman smiled and stood up. "It's so nice to meet you at last, Miss Travis. Peter will be surprised to learn you're here so early. He didn't expect you until late this evening. I'll tell him you're here," she said as she turned away from her desk.

Hensley buttoned her navy blazer as she stood waiting, wanting to look trim and unrumpled after the morning's drive.

"Hensley!" Peter's voice boomed a welcome as he came striding out of his office. He grabbed her hand in his strong grip. "Welcome . . . welcome, how was your trip?"

"Great—easy driving and everything went well. I enjoyed every minute of it. You can really barrel along through this 'big-sky' country of yours."

"And you must have done just that. You made the trip in record time." He still had a firm grip on her hand, and she liked the wide grin that spread across his tanned face. He paused, looking directly into her eyes. The silence held a bit of strangeness for her. Withdrawing her hand, she turned her face away from his steady gaze. It was foolish, but she felt warm and as if she might be blushing under his admiring scrutiny.

"I'll take you to lunch," he said, "and then I want you to have a look at an apartment Emma helped me find." Peter turned to his secretary. "Those letters will keep until this afternoon, Emma. Don't look for us before two-thirty."

He took Hensley's arm and propelled her out of the office, at the same time peppering her with words. "You know, I'm still curious as to what got you out here."

"I wanted to see the wide-open spaces of the Old West," she said lightly.

"That evasive answer matches the Mona Lisa look on your pretty face," he said, shaking his head in resignation. "But whatever the reason, I'm glad you decided to come."

"Me too." Now, out of the building, Peter's teasing words and warm manner dispelled the strangeness she had felt. Perhaps, she thought, it was observing Peter in his own setting that had awed her somewhat. Having always equated him with Allan, she saw him in a brotherly role. Seeing Peter in a suite of offices, head of a company bearing his name, did add a formidable dimension to his image.

As they sat at a table in a downtown café waiting for their lunch order, she felt at ease with him. "Tell me," she asked, "what was it you said about an apartment?"

"I'll take you to see it as soon as we've had our lunch. It's in the group where Emma Carlson lives. The only vacant one, and I was lucky to hear about it, thanks to Emma, of course. It's a good location; I took a look at it, and although it's not large, it may prove suitable for you." He shook his head. "I'm afraid our town doesn't offer a wide selection of apartments."

"I think this sounds good. I appreciate your scouting it out for me."

The waitress placed their salads in front of them. "Emma's doing, really," he said.

"I like her, Peter. She's very friendly," Hensley said, tearing cellophane from a package of crackers.

"She's indispensable." He chuckled. "And furthermore, she knows it! She worked for my dad and she's truly *my* right hand now. I'm lucky to have her in my corner."

Hensley stopped eating, looking over at Peter as he talked. Her attention was held by the genuine affection evident in Peter's tone as he spoke of his secretary.

"I was twenty-four when Dad died. I knew the copper business, but I felt far from ready to take control of the company. Fact is, I was scared to death.

Afraid I couldn't live up to my father's success with the business. Emma, bless her"—his eyes narrowed thoughtfully as he recalled that time—"was always there with a push and a pep talk. Why, she was like a football coach before a big game. She kept me revved up and carrying the ball without a fumble. Dad said she was as much a part of the company as if she'd been a Merrick herself." He smiled. "You'll see what I mean when you get to know her." He signaled the waitress for more coffee.

"I think she sounds like quite a lady, and I *want* to get to know her."

"Good, because she would like you to stay at her apartment until you get your own place and get settled."

"I'd like that." She felt pleased, hearing the plans that had been made to welcome her. "This Western hospitality is the greatest; I mean that." She smiled. She felt happy about having come. She settled down to eating her lunch in a state of euphoria.

Peter had already finished his salad and was attacking a steak sandwich with gusto. "Emma knew Allan, of course, so she was quite pleased to hear you had decided to take all my good advice and come to Anaconda." He kept the conversation between them going. "She was curious about you, asking all kinds of questions, the way you gals do."

She knew he was egging her on a bit, but she enjoyed it. "What questions did Emma ask?" she said. He had piqued her curiosity.

"First she asked me if you were a lot like Allan. I said not exactly, of course."

"What does that mean?"

"It means just what I told her." He paused to drink some more coffee. "Not exactly."

She realized he was doing this with deliberate slowness to tease her. This made her determined not to give him the satisfaction of prodding him to continue.

61

She watched as he took another swallow, and then another.

"You're exasperating, Peter," she said finally, unable to stand it any longer. "Stop teasing me and tell me what you told your secretary about me."

"I told Emma you were not only much smaller than the ol' miner, but a whole lot prettier!" He ogled her, suppressing laughter.

She shook her fist at him. "You're as big a tease as Allan was. I'm beginning to wonder if he learned these tactics from you, or you from him."

"That's a very debatable question, Hensley." Peter's dark eyes sobered. "The times that brother of yours and I had—they were the best." He looked away and raised his hand in a signal to the waitress. "I'll get the check and we'll go see the apartment," he said, changing the subject. She felt suddenly very much aware that her presence in Montana brought memories of Allan into sharp focus for Peter.

They drove in Hensley's car. Peter gave the directions, and she followed them easily. "You handle your car well," he said, "none of those distracting traits of most women drivers."

"You sound prejudiced against females at the wheel; are you?" She glanced at him out of the corner of her eye to see if he were serious or merely teasing her again.

"I admit it. I even make it a practice to avoid letting one get behind the steering wheel. You may prove to be my one exception," he said, giving her a complimentary salute. Before she could comment, he gave further instructions. "Around the next corner to the right and we'll be there, Hensley."

She slackened speed and pulled the car to a smooth stop in front of several groups of natural-stone-and-cedar-shake buildings. Away from the tree-lined street, the setting was shady and inviting. The apartments were grouped around an open courtyard with two upper-level and two lower-level apartments in each complex.

"The lower, in the far-left group, is Emma's." Peter pointed it out to her as they crossed the courtyard. "The one available for rent is the upper in this first complex to the right." He gestured, wagging his index finger as if he were conducting a sightseeing tour.

Climbing the short flight of stairs, Peter opened the door for her. They entered the living room, which had a dining area to one side. Beyond this an arched doorway gave a view of a small, compact kitchen. At the opposite end of the living room, a door led into a hall, off which was the one bedroom and bath.

Peter remained in the living room while Hensley scurried around emitting small sounds of pleasure. "The bedroom is almost spacious—big windows—so light and airy. Thank goodness this bathroom has white tile. I can use any color towels—the wilder the shade, the better. In Ironville the bathroom was tan—ugh—I hate yucky brown in a bathroom."

"I'll make a note of the fact," Peter hollered down the hall.

Hensley rejoined him. "I do like it. Did you happen to notice all the walls are oyster white? They were smart to decorate in white, then tenants with pet color peeves can't be offended."

"Like tan tile?" he said, obviously enjoying her enthusiastic approval of the place. "I take it all this means you do want to rent it?"

"I do if the price is right. You're the guardian of the till, so how about it? Can I afford the rent?" She stood facing him, her hands on her hips.

"You'll be glad to know it's forty dollars a month less than Allan's apartment in Ironville. I've already put up a deposit to hold it until you could see it. That's why I had the key handy in my pocket, in case you had wondered. Of course"—he grinned at her—"I will deduct my deposit from your first paycheck. See, I'm really a Scrooge of a boss!"

"Whatever you are, I don't care." She laughed. "I do like the apartment and it'll be perfect for me."

"Emma told me to tell you she had some furniture in storage, a few things she couldn't use when she moved from her house, and you're welcome to them. In fact, it will save her a storage bill, she said. Also, the ranch is loaded with chairs and chests of drawers, if you can use some." He shrugged. "One guy can't use them all."

"Great! Between you and Emma Carlson I can get settled in no time. I brought my only furnishings in the car with me: my stereo and my country-music albums." She smiled. "Couldn't leave them behind, you know."

He shook his head. "I'm not surprised. I heard all about your musical hang-ups from Allan." He feigned a look of distaste.

"Don't knock it, Peter, if you haven't tried it." She tilted her head, studying him with a calculating look. "I could introduce you to some country music I bet you'd enjoy."

"Not if I can avoid it, you won't," he said with a wry grimace. "Come on . . ." He gave her a push toward the door. "I've got to get back to work."

"Yes, and I need to find out about my job at the Merrick Copper Company," she said, quickly adopting a serious attitude. "I sure hope my limited business talents will be equal to the demands of your industry."

"Have no doubts," Peter said, following her out of the apartment. He closed the door and handed her the key. "You may discover you're a great deal like your brother. He was so fascinated with mining, he had iron ore in his blood. I'd like to think we may instill some of the magic of copper in you."

A certain quality in Peter's voice moved her. She did not respond to his words, but her lips parted in an inaudible sigh. She could almost hear Allan's voice telling her again the definition of Montana. "It's Spanish for 'mountain treasure'—the gold and the silver. And Peter will tell you it's 'copper', too."

Chapter 7

Settling into her apartment as well as into the pattern of her new job took Hensley's time and concentrated efforts for the next few weeks. In both places, Emma Carlson proved to be a motherly friend and adviser.

"I feel as if I'm commencing to put down roots and replant my life here in Montana," Hensley said to Emma. She had returned from a lunch hour spent shopping, and stopped at Emma's desk to show her the bedspread she had purchased on sale.

"You'll soon feel like your brother in that respect, Hensley. I believe he felt at home here."

"I know he did. It's funny, but Peter said something of the sort to me—that the mountains of Montana would give me the same sense of belonging as they had given to Allan." She smiled; "I like the thought," she said wistfully.

Catching sight of the digital clock on Emma's desk, Hensley gathered up her package. "Whoops! It's after one. I've got to get back to my desk." She hurried out, clutching the awkward bundle in her arms, colliding head-on with Peter.

"Hey!" He threw his arms out, grabbing the bedspread and her waist. "You're putting on a little weight there, aren't you?" He emphasized his little joke with a bear hug.

The awkwardness of the situation embarrassed her, more so because she felt very conscious of Peter's strong arms holding her securely. She looked up into his laughing face and for an absurd moment she had the insane idea he might be going to kiss her. Tremulous excitement spiraled through her as she imagined how Peter's lips would feel pressing hers. Her cheeks flamed.

As if he could read her mind, his dark eyes sparked in amusement and he hugged her again. "You know, Hensley, this is an awful wedge to put between friends, and it camouflages your lovely contours."

"I—I'm late," she stammered, glancing away from him in confusion and struggling to free herself.

"You need a flagman to signal a wide-load warning," he said, releasing her. He laughed aloud this time, obviously highly amused at her discomfort. "But you don't need to run off," he added as she took a step away from him.

"I do work here, you know," she said, trying to recover some shred of composure. "I need to get back to my desk." Turning, she walked away down the hall, affecting as dignified a retreat as she could manage.

Still laughing, Peter entered his outer office. "Young and exuberant girl, isn't she?" he said to Emma.

"Hensley? I think she's a pure delight," Emma stated emphatically.

Peter eyed his secretary with a look of speculation. "Uh—huh—and what is it you intend for me to read into those words exactly?" He continued to regard her with one eyebrow raised.

"Why,—not a thing—nothing." Putting her hand up, she patted her carefully styled gray hair in the feminine gesture Peter was accustomed to seeing. She then assumed her office voice. "Miss Lawrence telephoned, three times in fact. She asked that you return her call at your earliest convenience."

"Emma, you've mislaid your usual sublety," he baited her, knowing full well she found Margo's calls a nuisance. "Please, get her on the phone for me now and I'll take it in my office."

I'll have fun tonight, Hensley thought as she left work. She felt glad not to be spending Friday evening alone. She had accepted a date with Ray Holden, from the accounting department, and she was looking forward to it. Though a bit on the brash side, she found Ray good company. "I'm the most refreshing thing at Merrick Copper, next to the water cooler." She smiled thinking of this oft-repeated remark of Ray's. "And that's where you'll find me—next to the water cooler," he would always add. He did revel in being the center of attention wherever he was, she thought.

"Have you been to the Red Barn yet?" he had asked her when they made plans for this evening.

"No, I haven't," she told him, and this bit of news seemed to please him.

"I'm glad I'm the first one to take you, then. Anaconda doesn't boast any pretentious restaurants, but the motel on the highway to Butte has this dining and club room. Anaconda's best," he exclaimed, "good food served Western style."

Hensley and Ray arrived at the Red Barn at seven o'clock, and the dining room was already well filled. Flickering lights from wagon-wheel chandeliers cast an intimate glow over the shadowy interior. Rough-hewn wooden beams spanned the ceiling, and walls of the same rustic wood were decorated with a variety of black metal branding irons. They made their way among the red-cloth-covered tables to one for two near the far end of the long room. Nearby was a raised dais on which was placed a solitary stool made of split logs.

No sooner were they seated than a blue spotlight cast a halo of light on the blue-jean-clad figure of a bearded young man. He seated himself on the log stool and began to softly strum a guitar and sing.

My heart knows just regret—of a love I can't forget,
A love that faded and went wrong.
My days dawn sad and blue—empty, lonely too,
There's nowhere I belong.
The rains come every day, the music dies away, silencing my song.
The joy of love's refrain is over and the pain is all that lingers on.
I remember the delight—that once filled my lonely night,
With a love song.
Oh, my darling, I need you—and you know that it takes two,
To sing a heart-song.

Hensley did not take her eyes off the singer until the plaintive song ended. "You didn't tell me they had a country singer here!" she cried, applauding enthusiastically.

"I didn't know it. He's new, I guess," Ray said.

"He's very good. The song is lovely—I like it. I know I've never heard it before." She frowned, lacing her fingers in the loops of the gold chain around her neck. "I rather pride myself on my knowledge of country music and performers," she said, tugging at the chain thoughtfully. "I'd like to find out about him."

"My guess is the guy is local talent," Ray said, lighting a cigarette. He knew she didn't smoke, so he was careful to divert his smoke away from her. "Outside entertainment in these parts is limited to Butte at rodeo time," he added.

A waitress in a short denim skirt and red bandanna shirt interrupted them to take their dinner order.

Hensley made her selection without deliberation, and closing the menu, thrust it quickly aside. Her attention was again riveted on the entertainer. He had begun picking another melody on the strings of his guitar. It too was unfamiliar and caressed her ear with its pensive lyrics.

"Hensley, you're definitely bruising my ego!" Ray's voice reached out for her attention, and at the same time he nudged her foot under the table. "Am I going to have to get a *gee*tar to make points with you?"

She smiled quickly, sensing he was really miffed. She knew Ray was not one who cared to share the spotlight with anyone. "No, Ray, absolutely not. Why, you have a rampant charm that doesn't require music." Leaning forward she kept her eyes on him. "I've never been to a rodeo," she said, attempting to change the subject. "Tell me about the ones they have in Butte."

"They're great," Ray said, leaning toward her. "You'd get a thrill watching the steer riding. There's plenty of excitement and danger." His face was full of animation. "Next one that comes, you'll have to see it. Beats everything else for thrill-seeking," he said with a wide grin that showed his even teeth. "Guarantee you'll like bronc-busters as much as that singer." He winked, obviously pleased at having her complete attention now.

The waitress placed their steaks before them on sizzling platters; they concentrated on enjoying their dinner. The guitar player had taken a break, and Hensley smiled to herself, for Ray could relax now and stop trying to keep her from seeing or hearing anyone but him.

"Hey, look who just came **in**," Ray whispered, indicating two couples taking a table across the room. "The boss himself!"

Hensley glanced over to see Peter holding a chair for a striking-looking girl. She felt a twinge of envy, noting the way the girl's sleek black slacks and cowl-necked sweater set off her pale gold hair. "Who's the blond with Mr. Merrick? Do you know her?" She kept her voice low, trying to sound casual.

"She's Margo Lawrence, considered the reigning beauty of these parts. Quite a dish isn't she?" he drawled, then added a clicking sound of male approval to his words.

"Uh-huh," she admitted grudgingly.

"They say she's trying to put a bridle on Merrick. Of course, there's no denying Merrick money and Merrick charm are desirable commodities on today's market." He winked, making the clicking sound with his tongue again. "Wouldn't you agree?"

"I don't know. I suppose so." She looked down at her food and cut another bite of steak. For some inexplicable reason the face of Allan's girl flashed through her mind—Karen Blake, as beautiful in her dark, exotic way as this Margo Lawrence was in her shimmering blondness. She felt Ray watching her, so she said, "I'd have to say, they do make a good-looking couple." She shrugged to show her indifference. "Maybe they have the real thing going for them."

"Who knows?" Ray chuckled. "I find it hard to speculate on the executive level. Anyway, I don't go for her type." He reached across the table and covered Hensley's hand with his. "I prefer a certain pretty gal who digs country music myself."

"Well, I'm glad to hear it," she said, deliberately placing a flirtatious quality in her tone. They both laughed.

When the waitress appeared to refill their coffeecups, Ray excused himself, saying he wanted to get a fresh pack of cigarettes. However, instead of going in the direction of the cigarette machine, he approached the stage and spoke to the entertainer.

"I watched you, Ray. What were you up to?" Hensley asked when he returned to the table.

"You do think the singer is great, don't you?" He eyed her with a sly grin.

"Yes, of course I do, but—"

"I thought you'd like to tell him so. You've been wrapped up in his music most of the evening, although you've been mighty careful to listen to me with one ear while you heard that fellow's songs with the other." His grin was wider now. "I'm trying to score points. If you can't lick 'em"—he shrugged—"then join 'em, I say. The singer will come by the table on his next break."

Smiling, she said, "You're a nice guy, Ray Holden, and ingeniously thoughtful."

"Hi, I'm Craig Reilly," the young man said in answer to their introductions.

"We're thoroughly enjoying your music," Hensley said with enthusiasm. "How long have you been singing here?"

"I've worked at the motel since June, as a busboy mostly. Wasn't till the end of August I convinced them to give me a chance as an entertainer." He rubbed his bearded chin. "Now I perform during the dinner hour."

"We're glad we caught your act, Reilly," Ray said. "Hensley here is high on those songs of yours."

"They're original, aren't they?" she asked.

"Yes, ma'am; wrote 'em all myself." There was pride in his voice.

"You have something special." Hensley put an emphasis on each word. "You have a future in country music. I'd bet money on it!"

"That's what it takes, Miss Travis—money." He scratched his jaw. "Money and the breaks. And you can be sure I'm going to make a grab at it!" He narrowed his eyes, wagging his head slowly.

"I'd like very much to see your songs. How many have you written?" She spoke rapidly in her interest to learn what he had composed.

"Fifteen, maybe twenty—that I sing all the time, that is. I'm not real certain. Guess I never stopped long enough to count 'em." He laughed. "Can't show you any, 'cause they're stored in my head and fingers." He tossed his head back, then leaned forward in a kind of mock bow to her as he said, "You'll have to come here and listen to me play 'em."

"You need to get them written down, Craig." She pointed her finger at him, frowning. "Not only written, but copyrighted. Someone could steal your songs from you. You do realize that, don't you?" Her voice rose in agitation.

"No way, folks! I'll never let it happen. My songs are mine, and they're all I've got going for me."

"Then get the notes on paper as fast as you can!" She felt actual alarm for him. She wondered if he were aware of the extent of his talent.

"I don't know about writing musical notes," he admitted. "Never learned to read music, either." He shrugged with a show of unconcern. "Got to get back up front now, but I thank you both for your interest. Come hear me often, won't you?"

Ray shook Craig's hand and clapped him on the shoulder. "Best of luck to you."

"I'll come hear you often, but please, do at least get your original songs taped. I mean it," Hensley reiterated with a smile.

Craig Reilly returned to the stage, taking his position in the circle of blue light. Holding his guitar pressed against his body, he bent his head and let his supple fingers pick introductory chords, and then the clear tones of a melody followed. He tossed his head with a touch of dramatic flair and began to sing: "I travel a happy road—my love by my side to lighten my load—"

Snatches of Craig's melodies ran through Hensley's mind all Saturday morning as she dusted and vacuumed her apartment. She did not turn on her stereo, preferring to recall the songs she had heard last night rather than listen to her collection of country albums. How she would love to have a recording of the first song of his she had heard.

"My heart knows just regret—da-dada-da-da-da—to sing a heart-song . . ." She wished she knew the words. The melody had a quality of sadness about it, as if each note were a tear. She felt a tremor of loneliness, but she smothered it in activity. Pushing the sweeper rapidly, she covered the small remaining area of hall carpet.

It was a Saturday ritual for Emma to stop in for coffee about eleven o'clock as she returned from her weekly appointment at the beauty shop. Hensley pushed the remaining bits of Craig's songs from her thoughts and started to seek out a subtle device to get information about Margo Lawrence from Emma. Why did she have such a curiosity about Peter's date last night? she wondered. Was it what Ray had said about this girl wanting to hook Peter?

She unplugged the electric cord and wrapped it methodically through the brackets on the side of the vacuum cleaner, then pushed the sweeper into the hall closet. The apartment in order, she went into the bathroom to freshen her lipstick and run a comb through her hair before Emma arrived. Tying her hair back with a green scarf, she thought: I wonder how I would look with hair the color of corn silk like Peter's girl. She could see her own darker blond hair gave her face a healthy, conventional look. She wrinkled her nose. Like an ad for soap, I'm home-style butterscotch while she is creamy-rich divinity. "Damn," she said aloud. "I'm even 99 44/100 percent pure!"

"You're a devil to tempt me with that," Emma said, watching Hensley take coffee cake from the oven.

"I know, but we can both pass up lunch today,"

Hensley agreed as she cut wedges of the cinnamon-and-brown-sugar-topped cake and placed them on green-bordered china plates.

"You don't have to pass up anything, being both young and slender, but I possess neither of those traits." Emma sighed. "If you weren't my nicest neighbor, I'd hate you for this." She laughed in resignation. She carried the plates to the table while Hensley poured their coffee. "Heaven help me, it smells like it's filled with almonds, too. I'm totally ruined!"

Hensley put their coffee and the cream and sugar on the table as the phone rang. "Go ahead and eat this while it's hot, Emma, and I'll make this short." She reached for the telephone.

"That sounded rather interesting, what I gathered from your side of the conversation," Emma said a few minutes later as Hensley rejoined her.

"Um—nice, and something of a surprise as well. It was Peter. He asked me to drive to Butte with him tomorrow—wants to show me some copper mines, he said. Even mentioned taking me to dinner at the Red Barn after we get back, so I can hear the country-rock singer who entertains there."

"From that glow on your face, I'd say you were quite pleased at the prospect." Emma smiled at her and poured cream in her coffee.

"You bet I am. I really want to hear Craig Reilly's songs again."

"And don't you want to see the copper mines?"

Hensley looked up at Emma and frowned. "Sure I do. I need to know something about mining copper if I'm going to write about it." She popped a loose almond into her mouth. "But I bet Peter is exactly like Allan, feels everyone should want to delve into the earth's core. I'm not all that excited about huge holes in the ground. I remember the few times Allan took me to the Mesabi iron pits. It was dusty, and I guess I wasn't all that fascinated by iron."

"How about copper and Peter?" Emma probed, her gray eyes smiling.

She looked at Emma, her glance questioning. She was having difficulty shifting her thoughts; she was still thinking about Allan and the Mesabi mines. "What, Emma?" She blinked her eyes quickly. "What do you mean about Peter?"

"Nothing, really." She patted her newly set hair. "I'm glad Peter is taking you. I believe you two will enjoy the day together." Emma's lips curved in a caring smile.

Hensley gave her an affirmative nod and jumped up. "The coffee has cooled off; I'll get us some that's hot."

"Say, Hensley, do wear that green scarf around your hair tomorrow. That touch of green is exactly right with your hazel eyes."

Hensley hesitated in the kitchen doorway, her back toward Emma. She raised one hand and touched the scarf where it circled under her hair at the back of her neck. Emma's words struck a chord in her memory. It was exactly the sort of remark her mother used to make to her.

Chapter 8

The topaz rays of the October sun had already warmed the air and toasted the morning frost from the brown grass. Like tape unwinding, the highway stretched invitingly ahead. There was little traffic, as it was still the church hour.

Peter pulled a black-stemmed pipe from the pocket of his herringbone jacket. "Mind if I enjoy a pipe as I drive? If I open the ventilating window I don't think it will smoke up the car."

"Fine, go ahead. Matter of fact, I like the odor of good pipe tobacco." She glanced at him, smiling her approval. "You know, I don't recall seeing you with a pipe before."

"Probably not, I don't smoke regularly. I do enjoy it, however, when I'm driving and when I'm on the job at the mines or smelteries." He reached above the sun visor, pulling out a leather tobacco pouch. "Since you don't mind, hold the wheel a minute while I fill this."

"Let me do it for you," she said, taking the pipe and pouch from his hand. "I know how—really I do," she said in answer to his skeptical look. "I did it often for my dad, and I remember quite well how he liked it done." She could see clearly from Peter's expression that he doubted her abilities in this male area, so she had fun making a ceremony of the task. She gently pushed the bowl of the pipe into the pouch of tobacco, then packed the brier bowl firmly, using her forefinger as a tamper. Performing this action with precise care, she then, with a bit of flair, placed the pipe stem in Peter's mouth.

"Good job," he mumbled through his teeth while keeping a firm bite on the stem.

"Now, if you'll give me a match, I'll light it for you," she said. He searched his coat pocket and withdrew a book of matches, placing them in her outstretched hand.

Striking one, she waited for the flame to hold steady and the sulfur to burn off before holding the flame to the pipe. "Now, how's that?"

"Exceptional—never had it done better!" He winked at her, pocketing the matches and drawing on the pipe. "Say, you looked like you were enjoying the singer the other night. Saw you at the Red Barn with Ray Holden—he's a nice fellow—competent accountant too, been with the company three years now."

Peter's observations of all that had taken place surprised her. The fact that he knew all about Ray was to be expected. She imagined he kept himself informed about all of his employees. But she wondered how he had had time to note all the details about their meeting with Craig Reilly while seeming to be engrossed in entertaining his own friends. She found this intriguing somehow.

After his comments, she couldn't resist interjecting one of her own. "Your girl is very pretty," she said, making her voice matter-of-fact. "Quite as striking a blond as Allan's girl is a brunette."

Obviously her statement amazed Peter. Certainly it distracted him. The car slowed noticeably as he took his foot off the gas feed. "Whatever made you think of her? I didn't think you liked Karen Blake."

"I don't. I resent her bitterly. The fact does remain, however, that she is pretty, and so is your girl." Her voice sounded strained; she wished she had never mentioned any of this. "Let's not dwell on it," she said, clipping her words.

"You brought it up, Hensley," he reprimanded her. "Also, what gave you the idea Margo was *my* girl?"

She found his manner condescending and she made no attempt to hide her resentment. "Only making bright conversation," she flipped. "Let's forget it." Turning her head quickly, she concentrated her attention on the highway markers. "We must be almost to Butte, aren't we?"

"Well, she is not—and yes, we are."

It took her a second to comprehend his cryptic answer. She stared at him, her eyes widening, her defenses slipping away. She could see the corners of his dark eyes crinkling in withheld laughter as he watched her reactions. She couldn't keep from smiling. "Touché," she said.

Amicability restored between them, Peter began enumerating the sites he wanted to show her. "First, I want to take you to the copper mines. There are so many things I'd like to teach you about copper."

Gearing her mood to his affable one, she said, "I'll promise to be an attentive student."

"One surprising thing, Hensley. There are mines, literally, under the city of Butte; it's ore from these very mines we smelt in Anaconda." He emptied his pipe and deposited it on the dashboard.

"That's frightening! How could they mine under an actual inhabited place?"

"The mines are very deep, so for the most part people have never worried about the underground shafts." He rubbed his chin. "Maybe they just got used to the idea."

"If I lived there, I think I'd want to make sure they weren't mining right under my house, or way deep under me either." She hunched her shoulders in a shudder.

"Those veins have played out, at the present time. Now the ore comes from the open-pit mine. We'll be there in a few minutes."

Peter parked the car in an area as close as he could to the rim of the open-pit mine. "You're in for a lot of walking," he said, helping Hensley out of the car. "Better put on your sweater, it will be windy and cool." He buttoned his jacket as he spoke. Hensley pulled on the beige turtleneck sweater she had brought. The snug-fitting knit pulled the scarf from her hair as she tugged it over her head. Retying the scarf peasant style, to hold her hair more securely, she remembered it had been Emma's suggestion that she wear the green chiffon today. The thought amused her. She had her face entirely framed in green at the moment, and so what. Certainly no one was making anything of it.

As if she had voiced her thoughts, Peter commented, "This old mine never had a better-looking explorer, and I'm glad you got over the habit of hiding your pretty eyes behind dark glasses." His eyes were smiling but his tone was serious.

"I only wore them because I thought they made me look sexy."

"You're plenty sexy without adding sunglasses." He arched an eyebrow. "And it seems to me that all the men at Merrick Copper have noticed that fact."

She glanced at him quickly. Something in his tone of voice made him sound angry. He gave her a teasing look, but he did not smile. Instead, he tucked her arm through his and they walked away from the car.

As they approached the upper rim of the open pit, he measured his steps carefully to hers, staying close beside her. She gaped in wonder at the sight of the crater, for it looked like a tremendous sunken arena of terraced brown earth.

"It's huge—really unbelievable." She shook her head in awe.

"Would you believe it's more than a mile wide?"

"I certainly would—every bit of it," she agreed. "It's incredible."

"It's over a mile wide and at least fifteen hundred feet deep." He waved his arm to indicate the vast expanse.

"Besides being so immense, it's pretty because of those green stripes of color showing in the earth." She pointed around the sides of the pit.

"Those vertical areas of green are copper, Hensley, and to me there is no more beautiful sight." He squeezed her arm as he gazed out over the mine. "I'm glad you noticed. Shows you're my kind of girl."

She did not respond to his statement; she was too

busy wondering if he meant anything by it. Probably not, for he did not look at her, indeed was not paying any attention to her at all. He stood very still at her side, his eyes fixed on the areas of copper along the walls of the mine.

"All my life the moldy green color and the rough feel of the copper ore have been exciting to me. Furthermore"—he rubbed his finger back and forth beneath his nose—"I've even gotten so used to the sulfurous odor of the smelteries, it's not offensive to me."

She had been watching his face as he talked. "You know," she said now, "you get the same look when you talk about copper as Allan always did when he talked of mining the iron ore." She spoke quietly, but she had no sadness in her voice. "I should have paid more attention to Allan's mining stories and I wouldn't be such a greenhorn today."

She walked along the shoulder of the pit. "Whatever is that giant thing down there?" She stopped suddenly and peered down, pointing into the depths of the pit.

"That *thing,* my pet, is a shovel that scoops some fifteen cubic yards of earth at one bite. You see, they have to take off about two and a half tons of overburden to get a ton of ore." He shielded his face against the wind with one hand, clearing his throat before he continued explaining. "That's a whale of a lot of dirt; let me tell you!"

"What do they do with it all?" she asked, hugging herself now against the wind.

"Later I'll show you the trucks that haul it away." He took her arm as they walked ahead. "You won't believe it until you see it, but these trucks have wheels on them that tower taller than the height of two men."

They were walking along the edge now and Peter pointed out more of the copper veins to her. "Be careful, he cautioned. "This dirt is loose along here and

crumbles to dust under your feet. You could slip."
Putting his arm firmly around her waist, he guided her
steps carefully.

"Don't put such an idea in my head," she said. The
words were scarcely out of her mouth when she felt a
piece of ground shift beneath her left foot. "Peter!" she
screamed, lunging sideways.

Peter yanked her body hard against his chest, his
strong arms crushing her rib cage until she felt as if she
were encased in steel bands. She clung to him, her face
buried against the rough wool of his jacket.

"My God, Hensley!" He had his face against her
temple, and the harsh rasp of his voice hissed in her
ear. They stood clutched together for several minutes.
Then Peter began to pat her gently on the back.
"You're O.K.," he said reassuringly. "And there's
solid earth under your feet now." He pulled her
forward a few steps as he spoke, and now he lifted his
head. She felt a sharp stab of regret, for his warm
breath on her forehead had been a pleasant sensation.

"That really scared me." She was still trembling and
her voice shook.

"Don't worry. I'm not going to let go of you," he
said, easing his hold around her, but keeping one arm
circling her waist. "You put your arm around my waist
too. I intend to keep you safe and sound from here on."

There was no mistaking the concern in his voice, and
as they began to walk ahead, she realized that Peter had
carefully shortened his stride so his steps would match
hers perfectly. Hensley was acutely conscious that their
two bodies touched from shoulder to thigh as they
moved together. She wondered if Peter were as aware
of this as she. She deliberately kept her face straight
ahead, knowing full well her eyes would reveal the
extent to which his closeness was affecting her. How
lean and hard his body felt. She pressed her fingers into
the wool nap of his jacket.

The wind whipped at the free corners of her scarf, lifting her hair. The air was briskly cold, but at this moment she felt as warm as it she had been touched by sudden sunlight.

Several hours later, as they were driving back to Anaconda, Hensley questioned Peter about the beginnings of the Merrick Company. She enjoyed listening to him, for asking about copper was like drawing him out with a magnet.

"Dad had the first piece of copper ore from a Merrick-operated mine mounted for a paperweight. It always sat on his desk at the company. Remind me to show it to you next week at the office."

She heard the pride in his voice as he talked about the discovery of copper in the Anaconda area and his father's development of the Merrick Company. For the first time she was conscious of the look of compressed power in his angular jaw. He had a strong face that she found interesting and, she was forced to admit, exciting.

"You should see the smelteries. I'll have John Martin show you around, one morning next week."

She glanced away from his profile to pinpoint her attention to what he was saying. "I think I'd like that," she said quickly.

"Well, you may and you may not." He laughed. "You see, it's all true what they say about those ore-roasting ovens. They do belch fumes of sulfur and arsenic. Not an acceptable thought in these days of concern over air pollution."

"Yuk!" She wrinkled her nose in distaste. "You do draw a vivid, unpleasant picture. Sounds like a kind of volcano with a stifling odor." She held her nose. "That I can pass up."

He laughed at the face she was making. "It's not as bad as all that." Picking up his pipe, he laid it in her hand. "Now, I've just time for another smoke before we get to the Red Barn for dinner. Fill it for me again, please? I can tell you'd rather smell my Virginia tobacco mixture than contemplate the aroma of the smelteries."

"Any day of the week," she replied, promptly pressing tobacco into his pipe.

Craig Reilly acknowledged Hensley with a nod as she and Peter seated themselves at a table with a good view of the small stage. He then began to sing the song that had appealed to her the other night. "I remember the delight—that once filled the lonely night—with a love song—" She became immediately engrossed, listening to the words and watching Craig's fingers on the guitar frets.

"Hey, we haven't been here five minutes and already you've wrapped yourself up in a shell of country music. We did come to the Red Barn to eat, you know?" Peter handed her the menu with a bit of a flourish.

"It's that song. It says something to me." She swung her head slightly, keeping time with the music. "Certainly is Craig's style at his best."

"Ah, it's Craig already?" Peter teased her. "I should have known better than to bring you here. Allan warned me; he said country music and singers mesmerize you. How about turning a little of your rapt awe to this menu and me?"

Arching her eyebrows, she feigned a look of flattering absorption. "I will, sir," she said. "I'll do just that!"

He laughed. "That's much better."

Soon Craig came to their table and Hensley introduced him to Peter. When they asked him to join them he explained that he was expected to perform almost constantly while the dining room was filled.

"I just wanted to take a minute to say I've thought about what you said, Miss Travis. You know? Getting my songs written down and all? I sure want to do it, and I hoped maybe you knew someone I could get to help me." His mouth spread wide in an entreating smile as he directed his statements to Hensley.

"Why, I can help you if you borrow a piano somewhere." She ran her tongue across her lips. "Of course, it wouldn't be a professional job of scoring, I'm afraid, but it would be a step toward safeguarding your melodies."

"You mean that? You could help me?" He stood by the table looking down at her. "I'd be grateful to you." His dark eyes held hers. "I can't tell you how I'd appreciate it." He stroked his bearded chin. "No problem about a piano. I can arrange to use one here at the motel."

"Fine, we're all set, then. Call me during the day at the Merrick Copper Company. I work there, Craig. We'll find a time to get together and do the job." She smiled. "It will be fun."

"Sure it won't be too much trouble, now? I don't want to be a bother, ma'am," he drawled, his eyes still intent on her face.

"Not at all! Your songs are great; I'll enjoy getting to know them."

"I'll write one just for you. You bet I will! I'll give you a song for helping me."

The idea delighted her. "If you really mean it," she said, pressing her hands together in a light clapping sound, "it has to be one like my favorite. You were singing it just after we arrived tonight." She hummed a few bars.

" 'Heart-song'; if you like it, then it's yours! I'll give it to you," he said, and he rocked from side to side, squaring his shoulders rather like a boxer accepting plaudits due him for a winning bout. "When I make it to the top in Nashville," he added with a confident

84

smile. "I'll tell 'em all 'Heart-song' belongs to you, Miss Travis!" Without further words he turned and walked with a rolling swagger back to the stage.

Hensley realized suddenly that throughout her conversation with Craig, Peter had not interjected a single word. She looked at him, catching his disapproving expression.

"You don't share my enthusiasm for Craig's talents, do you?" she asked in a guarded voice.

Peter rubbed the bridge of his nose. "You know I'm not into country-rock music the way you are," he said cautiously. "Besides, you warned me once, as I well recall, not to knock it till I tried it." He kept his words light, but she could see he still frowned disparagingly.

"You don't approve of my helping him, then, is that it?" She was careful not to sound irriatated by Peter's attitude.

"I'm neither approving nor censuring." He put his arm on the table and tapped his fingers. "To be frank, I'm trying to figure out your singer friend. He's self-assertive and determined, and I'm sure it takes that and more to get recognition as a performer. I'd say he plans to get ahead at any cost."

"I'm certain he does too, but is that wrong?" There was no flippancy in her tone. She really was interested in Peter's opinions about Craig.

"That depends on the devices he uses to achieve his success, I'd say." He shook his head. "I somehow can't keep from wondering how he'll do it."

"My guess is, he'll do it on *wings of song*." She gave him an impish smile, unable to resist the cliché.

She saw Peter scowl at her. He opened his mouth slightly as if he were going to pursue the subject. Instead he clicked his tongue, then murmured, "Touché, my pet!"

It was close to midnight when they said good night at Hensley's door. "It's been a lovely Sunday, Peter.

From beginning to end, the nicest day I've had since coming to Anaconda." Reaching up on her tiptoes, she brushed his cheek lightly with her lips.

"What was that for?" he asked, taking her face between his hands and looking in her eyes.

"Oh, for . . . for thank you . . . and . . . for good night," she stammered. She was suddenly very aware of the caress of Peter's dark eyes.

"I like the idea," he said, smiling at her. "I enjoyed every minute of the day too, except for that scare you gave me at the mine." He put his hand under her chin, tilting her face up toward his. "You know, Hensley, there's a great deal more I want to show you. I believe Allan was entirely right in wanting you to try our Montana ways, and I'm glad you're finding that they suit you." He spoke slowly, all the time lightly tracing her cheeks with his fingers.

His hands felt excitingly warm; she was glad he was touching her. She felt suddenly light-headed. She drew in her breath in a tremulous sigh.

"You're cold," he said. "I should make you go inside." He moved his hand from her face, and she thought he was going to stop touching her. Involuntarily she swayed against him, at the same instant hearing his harsh intake of breath and feeling his arms tighten around her. His mouth covered her parted lips, tenderly at first as if he intended only a light caress to match the one she had given him. As the pressure of his arms increased, she felt her soft flesh being molded to the unyielding contours of his lean, rugged body. Peter's kiss was far from the light, fleeting one hers had been, and all her nerves and senses were made vibrantly alive under the golden heat of his embrace. There was no controlling the rise and fall of her breasts as the rapid acceleration of her heart raced to match the solid pounding in Peter's chest.

With the same suddenness with which it began, Peter

dropped his arms and eased Hensley from his embrace. Only his eyes held her now, and she was confused by the puzzled, questioning look she saw in them. What did it mean? Was Peter questioning her reaction or his own?

"Thank you—and good night." He repeated the words she had used earlier, but coming from him they sounded strange, almost as if he were angry.

He turned then, leaving her quickly, taking the steps to the lower level two at a time. When he reached the center of the dimly lighted courtyard below, he paused. Was he going to turn around, come back to her? Hensley's heart raced at the possibility. Surely, at least, he would look up to see if she were watching him. Even in the pale light she could see the rigid line of his back and the firm set of his broad shoulders. He hesitated for a long moment; then, without a backward glance, he strode out of the courtyard toward the street.

Hensley stood motionless, a myriad of thoughts encompassing her. What had she done? Why had Peter suddenly shown this odd ambivalence toward her? She could not understand him. Always before, she had thought of Peter in terms of Allan. He was her brother's friend, college roommate and fellow engineer. They were two men with the same interests. They were very much alike, Peter and Allan, weren't they? She frowned. There was, of course, one quite significant difference. Her lips quivered in a smile. Peter Merrick was, after all, not her brother.

She turned the key in the lock and entered the apartment. Why was she making so much of this? She shrugged. It really wasn't complicated. Peter had been her brother's friend, and now he was hers. It was that simple. There was no cause for her to make something monumental out of a day of sightseeing and a goodnight kiss.

She left a lamp burning in the living room and walked to the bedroom to undress. It was after midnight, and she had to be at work at eight in the morning. She had better stop thinking about Peter and the day's happenings and get to bed.

The silence in the apartment depressed her. It was so lonely coming home to an empty apartment, lonely and so quiet. She hummed a few notes of Craig's song, then filled in the words. "My days dawn sad and blue—empty, lonely too—there's nowhere I belong." She shivered. Was there nowhere she belonged? Allan had wanted her to come to Montana. Did she belong here? Certainly she felt more a part of things here than she had in Ironville—and yet . . .

Hanging up her clothes, she took a pair of blue pajamas from a drawer, putting them on quickly. Hugging herself, she rubbed her arms briskly. It was cold in the bedroom. Not just cold, but quiet, and she felt a hollow emptiness around her. Her life was empty without Allan. She missed him desperately.

Once today, at the open-pit mine, it had seemed almost as if he were standing there beside her. Maybe it was because when Peter had talked so excitedly about the copper ore, it reminded her of Allan and the times he had taken her to the Mesabi mines.

I hate living by myself, she thought, and for some reason she felt more alone tonight than usual. Tonight was like one of those first nights after Allan's funeral when she had realized she was totally alone, the last remaining member of her family. She heard a sudden low rumble of thunder. The sound was as mournful as her thoughts.

"I am a lone survivor." She closed her lips over the words and there was a salty taste in her mouth. She was crying, and the tears had wet her cheeks. Rubbing her face with a tissue, she climbed into bed and pulled the blanket over her shoulders. She lay still, listening to the pulsating of the raindrops against the bedroom window.

"The rains come every day—the music dies away—silencing my song." The poignant words of "Heartsong" and the sound of the rain melded in her mind.

Chapter 9

The following week, Hensley and Craig began the task of transcribing the sounds of his guitar strings into notes written on musical staff paper. Craig had only one day off a week from his work at the motel, and that day, Monday, didn't coincide with Hensley's work schedule. They worked together on Monday evenings and on Saturday and Sunday mornings before Craig reported to work at noon. Because of his late evening hours entertaining on the weekends, he didn't have to report for work early those two days. Then, too, these morning hours were a quiet time at the motel and Craig had no trouble arranging for the use of the piano.

"I wish I'd practiced more and paid attention to the musical theory my long-suffering piano teacher tried to instill in me," Hensley said to Craig during one of their early sessions. "I'm so darn slow. It takes me an eternity to get the timing right."

"You'll never hear me complain," he said, flashing a smile. "You're great and you make my songs sound better on that piano than they do on my guitar!" He winked at her. "And you know how I feel about top billing."

"I also know you hand out large servings of flattery,"

she countered. "Now, let me hear those last four notes again." She picked up her pencil, and leaning over the piano keys, she drew more notes on the lined paper.

As the music progressed note by note, Hensley attempted to learn a few facts about this purposeful man. "Where are your parents, Craig? Do they live in Montana?"

"They're dead," he stated without emotion. "I have an aunt in South Dakota. I lived with her while I was going to high school." He did not elaborate, and she stopped probing him about his personal history. His attitude indicated to her that his past was unimportant. The only subject he did discuss with any show of candor was his career and the goals he had set for himself. He seemed obsessed with the desire to go to Nashville.

While they worked, she listened to Craig tell of the success he was convinced he would enjoy in the country-music center. She found his fervor exhilarating. He was so sure his success was inevitable and he made her believe it too.

Watching him as he slowly picked a thread of melody from his guitar strings so she could score each note, she felt a twinge of envy. She wished she had such clear-cut goals outlined for her own life. What exactly did she want? She wondered if that question had not been lying dormant in her mind for some time. Now that it surfaced in her consciousness, she realized the answer. She wanted to discover a pattern for her life. Choose it—seek it—reach out and take it—as Craig was doing!

She had been staring at her hands on the keyboard. Now she scored the notes Craig had just played, sounded chords of harmony and then played it back. Together they ran through it a second time, Craig blending his guitar with her piano. When she was certain she had the tempo as he wanted it she ended with a glissando and closed the lid over the keyboard.

"That does it, Craig. Now I've got to call it a night

and get home." She smiled and yawned at the same time. "We worked late tonight," she said, moving away from the piano.

"I hate to see you drive home alone. How about letting me go along with you?" He held her coat as she slipped her arms in the sleeves.

"No need for that." She lifted her hair over her coat collar.

"I'm willing to oblige, ma'am," Craig drawled. "Fact is, I'm even more than willing. I'm eager!"

Hensley glanced at him. The innuendo beneath his humor took her by surprise.

He eyed her, allowing a slow grin to spread across his face.

She looked away from his eyes and busied herself with buttoning her coat and belting it snugly. The way he was watching her made her uncomfortable. She made no response.

"Well, if I can't do more for you, I can see you to your car." He put an arm around her shoulders, walking beside her toward the door.

A blast of cold air slapped across her face as they left the motel. Hensley lowered her head, hiding her face from the wind in the collar of her coat. She welcomed the distraction of the November weather.

He opened the car door for her. "You're not like any of the girls I've known before," he said as she slid in the driver's seat. "You're a very classy lady!" He narrowed his eyes, his expression sober. He kissed her quickly on the forehead; then, withdrawing his head, he closed the car door.

She turned the key in the ignition, backed out of the parking place and drove away. She could still feel the prickling sensation on her skin where Craig's beard had brushed her face. "A very classy lady." She shook her head. Now, exactly what was the connotation of that? she wondered.

Two days before Thanksgiving, Craig called her at the office. "I had to call you first thing, Hensley. I've got some great news!" She could hear the excitement in his voice. "I get to sing at the rodeo in Cheyenne! It's four days—early in December. One of their scheduled entertainers canceled out—they offered me the chance to substitute."

"Craig, that's marvelous!"

"Is it ever! It's a really big chance for me. There'll be entertainers from all the Western states—maybe agents, too." He poured out words in a torrent of enthusiasm. "My boss here is letting me take a week off to go to Cheyenne. I know something will come of this. I feel it. And thanks to you I have all my songs to take with me. You sure brought me luck, classy lady." He laughed. "You're better than a good-luck horseshoe."

"I'll take that last as a compliment," she retorted gaily. "Or is that your way of letting me know I've been a *nag* about getting your music written?" She laughed. She felt really happy for Craig. Too, she had a good feeling knowing she had given him some aid in his career. He had needed her help; she liked being needed. All my life I've leaned on others, she thought. Now, for the first time, someone is leaning on me. She found it gave her a sense of satisfaction.

She had been finishing an article when Craig called. Now she turned her attention back to it, typing the final paragraph. After a rapid proofreading, she put a paper clip on the left corner. She had a good feeling about this piece, knowing it was her best effort to date. She needed to get Peter's approval, for it should be in the mail to the trade journal before the Thanksgiving holiday.

Emma greeted her with an affectionate smile as Hensley approached the older woman's desk. "Looks like you've been working hard," she said, indicating the papers Hensley was carrying.

She nodded. "Could you ask him to look this over?"

she pointed toward Peter's office. "I should mail it today if Peter gives me the go-ahead."

"Oh?" Emma said with a light pat at her hair, reaching for her telephone. "Why don't you just take it in yourself? He's not busy, and"—she put her finger on the dial—"I do have a call I need to make."

Hensley had the fleeting impression that Emma was shooing her like a mother hen, especially when she added, "Go ahead, dear."

Hensley hesitated, pulling the cuffs of her long-sleeved blouse down over her wrists. Vague feelings of uneasiness made her want to stall a few minutes and muster up a facade of businesslike composure. She had had no occasion to see or talk to Peter, beyond a quick greeting when they passed one another in the halls here at the company, since the Sunday when he had taken her to the copper mine in Butte. Since he made no reference to what had happened between them, she supposed that he either had forgotten it or that he wanted her to forget it. Either way, she had no intention of attaching undue importance to the day. After all, she had been kissed before. Quickly she adjusted her collar at the back of her neck and walked through the door into Peter's office.

"Why, Hensley, I'm really glad to see you. I think you may have been hiding from me." He rose quickly from his desk, smiling at her as she entered.

What a marvelous smile he has, she thought, watching it broaden into a grin of welcome which circled his face, easing the rugged angles of his stern jaw. Feeling a flicker of self-consciousness because she knew she had been staring at him, she lowered her eyes. What had gotten into her? She certainly was overreacting to a simple male smile. A sudden odd realization struck her. Why, Emma had pushed her in her to confront Peter. She had not been busy at all and undoubtedly had even manufactured the urgency of a telephone call.

"Not hiding, just busy at my job," she said, hoping

her embarrassment did not show in her voice. Honestly, did Emma think she wanted to see Peter at every possible opportunity? Was Emma, in her maternal fashion, pushing her at Peter? She felt so warm that she knew her face must be flushed.

Peter appeared unaware of her discomfort, and she was grateful for this. He came toward her from behind his desk. "Good, I see you brought your article." He took the manuscript from her hand. "I'll look it over after lunch and return it to you."

Swinging around, he placed the papers on his desk, dismissing this bit of business with executive competence. Quickly he turned back to her. "I'm so glad you came in; I was planning on talking to you today. Now, sit down and tell me how your musical venture is progressing with young Reilly."

"Fine, actually it's finished. I just need to do some final scoring in ink."

"Good, then I hope you'll be free to spend the Saturday after Thanksgiving with me. You've never been out to the ranch, and I think you might enjoy a ride. Allan always took a tour of the place on Copper Belle. She's spirited, but an obedient mare." He leaned toward her. "You're frowning like the idea of riding one of my horses is not too appealing."

"No, no, it's not that." She put her hand to her forehead, rubbing the frown wrinkles. "I didn't follow you at first. I guess I was still thinking about Craig's songs." She shook her head. "I'm kind of distracted today," she added, and laughed.

"My fault; I did jump right from your music man onto my horse without benefit of a toehold in the stirrup, didn't I?" Leaning back in his chair, he rested his chin on his hand, eyeing her thoughtfully. "You do like to ride, don't you?" he asked.

"I used to, but I have to admit it's been a while." She paused. She hoped he would not be disappointed in her answer. "To be honest, I haven't been on a horse since I went to a summer camp in Minnesota at least ten summers ago. If you guarantee your Copper Belle isn't too frisky for a novice to handle," she added quickly, "then it's a date for Saturday."

"Great!" he said, and Hensley was relieved by the pleased tone of his voice. "I've been wanting to get you out to see the ranch before we get into real winter weather, but there hasn't been time before now. You've been wrapped up in your country singer, you know," he teased.

"For heaven's sake," she scoffed. "I wish you'd stop referring to Craig as *my* anything! I've enjoyed helping him, that's all. It's been fun."

"For you maybe, but it's more than fun and guitar strings to that song hustler!"

She could hear the undisguised antagonism in his tone. Why would Peter say these things? Craig Reilly was no possible concern of his. Why, she wondered, did he make such a point of how much time she had spent helping him? She found Peter's attitude to be patronizing, and it annoyed her that he thought she was that naive where Craig was concerned.

"I believe I'm better qualified than you are to judge the *song hustler*, as you call him," she snapped. "After all, I've been working with him for a month now and you've only heard him sing a few times at the Red Barn. He's a talented musician and I'm glad he needed my help. The whole experience has proven a pleasant change for me." She bristled with defiance. "I like the feeling of being needed for once in my life!"

"*Wow!* Whatever did I say to bring all that on?" he asked, running his hand through his hair, then rubbing the back of his head. "Believe me, Hensley, I had no intention of starting an argument. In fact, the last thing I want to do is fight with you, little girl!" He shook his head. "I only meant I was glad you were now free to spend some time with me." His eyes held an amused smile.

She jumped up from her chair. "And don't call me *little girl!*" She glared at him. "I must say, I don't like your condescending attitude."

The smile vanished from his eyes. He studied her in silence. "Look," he said quietly, his tone completely serious now. "I'm sorry I made you so angry. You performed a generous, friendly service for that singer. I'm not intending to belittle your actions. You will have to admit, however, it was most opportune for him when you happened along."

She allowed a smile to soften the tight lines around her mouth. "You need to understand how important it was for me to have someone to help, Peter. This is a rather new experience for me. Always before, I've leaned on others. I've certainly leaned on you, so for that reason"—she made a little contrite face—"I guess I should not be surprised if you refer to me as *little girl.*" She turned away. "Allan told me to seek your help, take your advice and of course depend on your guidance about money matters." She sighed. "I realize all this amounts to a great deal of leaning on my part."

He went to her, putting his hand on her arm. "Whatever it amounts to—I like it." He cupped her chin, tilting her face toward his. "I like your leaning on me, Hensley."

The warm look in his eyes gave her a soft, melting feeling. She moved against him, wanting nothing so much as to have him kiss her.

The intercom squawked a jarring interruption, abruptly destroying this fragile moment between them. She caught her breath, experiencing a stab of regret as Peter removed his hand from her chin. Clasping her hands together, she struggled to regain her composure as Peter walked away from her toward his desk. He flipped the intercom button and immediately Emma's crisp words announced, "Miss Lawrence is here for your luncheon appointment, Mr. Merrick."

"Thank you, Emma." He hesitated, shifting his

position. Hensley thought he glanced at her, but his movement was so quick it was imperceptible. "Ask her to come in," he said. Straightening, he addressed Hensley. "Margo is here; I want you two to meet. She knew Allan, of course, so she knows a little about you." His tone was easy, casual.

She got the impression that Peter was setting the stage, possibly trying to put her at ease. If that was his intention, he had failed. At this moment she felt as uncertain and as out-of-place as an alien traveling with a forged passport. Peter's words—"she knew Allan *of course*"—stung her ears. Why, the "of course"? Was Margo such an established part of Peter's existence that Allan would have had occasion to see her often—to know her well? Was this the implication of Peter's words?

Margo Lawrence moved gracefully through the office door, displaying flawless perfection of makeup and dress. At the sight of her, Hensley felt shapeless and utilitarian standing there in her beige skirt and simple blouse.

"Margo, I want you to meet Allan's sister, Hensley." Peter made the introductions with impartial candor.

"It's so nice to meet you. Ever since Peter told me you had moved here from Minnesota, I've been hoping we could get acquainted." Her low-pitched voice had a warm vibrant quality that Hensley had to admit was pleasing. "How do you like our big-sky country?" she asked with a show of genuine interest.

"I like it very much indeed!" Hensley tried to match Margo's friendly manner. "I'm beginning to understand the fascination Montana held for Allan. He felt no other place could compare with it."

"And your job—is this boss of yours as great to work for as I imagine he would be?" Margo directed her words to include Peter with a *soupcon* of coquetry.

"I'm learning the exciting facets of the copper industry and I like it," she said. "And no one is better

97

qualified to teach me than my boss." She managed a smile. "So, you're right, Margo, he is great to work for, but if I hope to remain on the payroll, I had better get back to my desk," she saluted Peter with a slight toss of her head and added, "I'll pick up the article I brought in after you've had an opportunity to look it over." With a few parting amenities to Margo, she hurried from the office.

Approaching Emma's desk, Hensley was conscious of her friend's covert glances. She knew Emma was surreptitiously studying her to determine her reactions to the meeting with Margo Lawrence. Hensley had no intention of giving the older woman the idea that she cared one whit who Peter took to lunch, or anyplace else for that matter. With deliberate nonchalance she paused, resting her fingers lightly on the corner of Emma's desk. "I'll check with you later this afternoon and pick up the article after Peter checks it over," she said, her tone as casual and unconcerned as she could make it. "See you later." Affecting a slight saunter, she walked out of the office, not waiting for Emma to interject any of her pointed comments.

Chapter 10

The wan light of the early-morning sun crept around the edges of the gray sky, offering no promise of brightness to the bleak day. Hensley found that not only the sight of this Thanksgiving day, but also its sounds, added to her depression. The chill November wind had increased through the night, and now gusts whirred around the windows. Outside, blasts of icy air whooshed across the courtyard like tennis balls volleying from rackets.

It was a holiday, her first one without her brother. Hensley realized she was allowing herself to build up a first-class case of the blues. Thank goodness she would be going over to Emma's this afternoon. If Emma had not asked her for Thanksgiving dinner—if she had had to eat alone—she would really have dissolved in a sea of self-pity. Holidays were family days, but she had no family now. She banged the cupboard door shut after she took out a glass for orange juice and a mug for coffee. She really did not want much breakfast, and she wanted to have plenty of time to bake a pie before she bathed and dressed for the day.

Surely Peter would telephone this morning. Deep down, she knew she had fully expected him to ask her to have Thanksgiving dinner with him. He, of all people, knew how this day could be for her—how sad and alone she would feel on this first Thanksgiving since Allan died.

Yesterday when Emma had mentioned the two of them getting together for dinner today she had amended her invitation, saying, "I'd be glad to ask your friend from the accounting department, if you'd like to have him join us. I thought of asking Peter, but he'll be having dinner with Margo and her family, I'm sure. That seems to have developed into a set pattern for him the past few years."

Emma's knowledge of Peter's plans upset her, there was no denying it. Ray Holden, of course, had told her over a week ago that he was going to Idaho to his married sister's for the holdiay weekend. She got out flour, shortening and the rolling pin. If she concentrated on baking a pie she'd work herself out of her despondent mood. She had indulged in feeling sorry for herself long enough.

It was noon when she took the pumpkin pie from the oven. The spicy aroma of cinnamon and cloves floated deliciously through the small kitchen. She smiled for the first time that day. The pie looked perfect with its fluted crust. She pursed her lips in satisfied pride. That pie will impress Emma, she thought as she placed her fragrant creation on a rack to cool. Deciding to wait to whip the cream for the topping until she got to Emma's, she went into the bedroom to dress.

"Your table is beautiful," Hensley said, admiring the cornucopia of fresh fruits and nuts Emma had arranged for a centerpiece, flanked by a pair of yellow candles set in low silver holders. Emma paused to light the tapers. It took just a second for the flames to lengthen and begin to burn with a steady glow. "That's the perfect touch," Hensley complimented her further, watching the reflection of the candles make mirrors of the crystal water goblets.

Emma's face glowed with pleasure. "If you'll fill the glasses, we'll be ready for dinner," she said, disappearing into the kitchen. In a few minutes she emerged bearing an oval platter with a plump, golden-brown roast chicken. "The turkeys were entirely too large for two of us," she said, as if apologizing.

"That hen looks superb and exactly the right size," Hensley said, taking her place at the table. "I'm starved!"

"I've been saving calories all day so I can enjoy every gluttonous bite." Emma laughed and began to carve slices of white meat.

Hensley looked at her friend's contented expression. How kind and nice she is, she thought. How comfortable it is to be here enjoying Thanksgiving with her. She smiled inwardly, and for a precious fleeting moment shewondered if her mother might not have been very much like Emma Carlson.

After they finished dinner and the dishes, Hensley kicked off her shoes and, tucking her feet under her, lounged contentedly on the love seat. Emma relaxed across from her in her favorite chintz wing chair.

"I feel indulged and happy and the best I've felt all day," Hensley purred. "I don't know why I allowed myself to get down in the dumps earlier, but I did sing the blues for a few hours. I even felt put out because Peter hadn't called to wish me a pleasant Thanksgiving."

Emma evidenced interest at the mention of Peter. Leaning forward, she rested her hands on her knees. "Did you stop to wonder why you felt Peter had neglected you?"

"Why, no—should I have?"

"It seems indicative of something to me," Emma stated assuredly.

Hensley frowned. "I know you're baiting me, but I'll go along and ask. What could it be indicative of except a bad disposition on my part?"

"I believe you have expected Peter to take Allan's place. Be your big brother, so to speak," she said gently.

"I don't know—maybe I have." She squirmed around, stretching her legs and swinging them over the edge of the love seat. "But it's because that's the way Peter sees me—as Allan's little sister."

"You see yourself that way, Hensley, because it's easier for you that way. There are no pressures. Isn't that right?" Emma's voice prodded softly.

"What are you driving at?" She narrowed her eyes, baffled by the curious slant of this conversation. "I feel like you're talking to me in riddles that I should know the answers to and don't."

Emma rested her head against the high back of the wing chair. "I'm saying, Hensley, you choose this role for yourself in order to keep from being involved. Think about it a minute. Isn't that why you left

Ironville? Didn't you find yourself involved in a situation you weren't ready to handle?"

Hensley's eyes widened in an incredulous look. "How on earth did you know that?" Her voice rose in disbelief. "Why—why," she sputtered, "I never talked to anyone about my reasons for leaving Ironville."

"Of course you didn't, but from some statements Peter made I put two and two together. When he returned from your brother's funeral, he mentioned your job at the newspaper. It seemed quite obvious to him that this man you worked for had more than an employer-employee interest in you. Peter wondered if you were completely aware of it."

"Well, Peter was very observant," she admitted with reluctance. Interlocking her fingers, she held them against her chin as she talked. "After Allan died, I was not only lonely, but possibly overly vulnerable. I'm not really sure. Everything was different for me somehow." She lowered her head, not wanting to meet Emma's appraising look. "My feelings for David were not deep enough to include any commitment. I realized it and I left. To compound the issue, David was not yet divorced, and you're right"—she lifted her head and now looked squarely at Emma—"I was not ready to become involved with a married man. Give me credit for that!"

Emma returned her steady gaze. "And what about becoming involved with a man who is not married?" she said pointedly.

"If you mean Peter—and of course you do!—well, I was under the distinct impression that he was already involved with Margo Lawrence. More than likely he intends to marry her."

Emma leaned forward. "Would you mind if he did—marry Margo, I mean?"

The question was unexpected, and she could feel Emma's searching eyes penetrate the thin mask of indifference she was attempting to place on her emotions. "This conversation is silly—absurd actually," she sputtered. "I honestly don't know how we got off on such a tangent." She attempted a little laugh. "Furthermore"—she shrugged—"to answer your ridiculous question, I have no reactions one way or another about who Peter chooses to marry. I—haven't exactly given the subject much thought."

"Then do, Hensley. Do think about it," Emma said quietly. She lifted her hand to fluff her hair, at the same time smiling warmly at Hensley.

Observing this familiar gesture of Emma's, she began to laugh. "You are an incorrigible matchmaker, you know that, don't you?" Emma laughed too, and it added comic relief that Hensley welcomed. She had sensed before this evening that Emma for some reason was not fond of Margo. She wondered what could lie behind this attitude. Margo was certainly attractive and charming enough for everyone to find pleasing, wasn't she? Her age and her background corresponded with Peter's. Truly they appeared well-suited to each other. Emma's question was beginning to bother her. Would she mind if Peter decided to marry Margo? Possibly she would—probably, if she let herself think about it. She shook her head to push away the thought. Emma was devious, but surely she meant well?

It was eight o'clock when she returned to her own apartment. She realized that she still clung to the hope that she would hear from Peter. All day she had been expecting him to at least call, and Emma's conversation had pushed him to the front of her thoughts again. She put some albums on the stereo. She needed to do something to help her unwind. She had ambivalent feelings about the entire day, and Emma had certainly planted a seed in a fertile area of her mind, where it was already beginning to grow.

She adjusted the volume on the stereo as the phone

rang. That will be Peter at last, she thought, and feelings of delight and relief surged through her, echoing in her voice as she answered.

"Hello—oh . . . ," She caught her breath, trying to hide the stab of disappointment. "Why, David—what a surprise!"

"Nice—I hope?" David's voice boomed.

"Of course, a very nice surprise. I just hadn't expected a long-distance call. How—how are you?" She searched for words to cover her confusion.

"I'm fine, but I wanted to make sure your Thanksgiving was a happy one."

The concern in his voice touched her. She was really pleased he had shown this thoughtfulness, and as he talked of Ironville and questioned her about her work and life in Anaconda, she felt good. His voice was so filled with his usual vigor, she could picture him tossing his red head as he talked loudly.

"I've missed you, you know. I'd really like to see you. How about coming to Ironville for Christmas? I'll make plane reservations and mail you the ticket."

"Oh, David—you know I can't do that."

"Yeah—I guess I do." She heard his good-natured chuckle. "But you can't blame me for trying!" He hesitated. "Say, I'm planning on making a stamp meeting and auction in Denver late in February. I'd like to come on to Montana and see you for a couple of days, if you'll let me."

"Let you? I'll be counting on it," she said with affectionate enthusiasm. She smiled to herself, thinking that this conversation was somewhat out of character for him. The old David, who always issued orders and stated his intentions as indisputable facts, now using finesse? She had to admit this tactic hit a responsive chord in her.

After talking to David, she kicked off her shoes and walked over to turn up the sound on the record player.

At least David had thought of her today. It was now apparent that he and Emma were the only ones who had thought of her on this holiday. Most certainly Peter had not. Well, why should he? He was involved with Margo, and certainly that seemed to be the way he wanted it. She thought of the conversation with Emma. She would like to damn her and bless her at the same time. Emma had forced her to probe her feelings about Peter, and tonight she was in no mood to sort through her emotions further. She would get undressed and watch television in her robe. She would not allow herself to end the day depressed. It was just that she had hoped Peter would think about her once today and let her know it mattered to him how she spent this particular Thanksgiving, her first one in Montana. She closed her eyes, knowing she had expected too much.

There were three quick raps at her door. She spun around, startled. The knocking sounded again, more sharply. "Hensley—Hensley! It's Peter—are you still up in there?" Padding across the room in her stocking feet, she unlocked the door. Elation swept through her. Peter had not let the holiday end without seeing her. As she opened the door to see him leaning on the door frame smiling at her, it suddenly seemed as if she had willed it to happen, that like Aladdin she had rubbed her magic lamp and caused her genie to appear.

"Forgive me for barging in so late," he said quickly. "I'll just stay a minute. I was on my way out to the ranch when I heard on the car radio that there's a chance of snow moving in by Saturday. So I thought I'd run by and see if you could make it for our ride around my place tomorrow. If we do get snow on Saturday, we'd have to miss our date otherwise." His smile widened. "I couldn't let that happen, you know!"

"Sure, Peter, tomorrow is fine." She ushered him in and closed the door behind him. "Sit down, you can stay a minute." She walked to the couch and sat down, tucking her stocking-covered feet under her. Peter tossed his coat over the back of a lounge chair and then joined her on the couch.

"How was your day, Hensley? I thought about you and I hoped it was a nice Thanksgiving for you." He took her hand, holding it tightly in his, his dark eyes filled with concern. Why, Peter *was* worried about me, Hensley thought. He did remember this was my first holiday without any family; I knew he would.

Aloud she said, "I went to Emma's for dinner, and it was lovely. You would be astounded at the abundance of good food we had. Emma's fuming that now she'll have to diet for a week to get even again." She laughed. "I probably should join her."

"That sounds like Emma. I'm sure glad you two got together." Peter searched his coat pocket for his pipe and tobacco. "She likes you a lot, Hensley."

"And I like her too! She's a wise friend, you know that?"

"Do I ever! But if you ever tell her that I admitted it"—he grinned "—I swear to you I'll deny it! Emma is the matriarch of the Merrick Company now, and I have to try to make her think I'm boss even when she's managing and advising!" He chewed his pipe stem, and while this action accented the stubborn jut of his jaw, there was a glint of resigned laughter evident in his dark eyes.

"Emma even had some advice for me today. Probably very good, and I may even take it, but first I need to think about it some."

"My, sounds weighty. Don't let Emma snow you!"

She let her glance move around the room and rest momentarily upon familiar objects in an unseeing stare. She blinked finally and continued her conversation with Peter. "I don't think Emma was trying anything like a snow job, Peter. But tonight I got the strange notion that perhaps she had an insight into my feelings. I might

add that these were feelings I didn't even dream I had."
She paused, shaking her head slightly. "I have to admit
when all this grabbed me, I felt more than a little
shook up."

"Sounds mysterious to me. You two must have had a
real soul-searching evening." She felt Peter's eyes on
her and sensed he was more than a little curious. She
had an instant, uncontrollable urge to question him.

"How do you see me, Peter?" she blurted out.
"Who—and what—would you say I am?"

"That's a hell of a loaded question." He laughed,
and laid his pipe in the crystal ashtray on the coffee
table in front of him. "I'd say without fear of contradic-
tion that you're an extremely exuberant girl with
marvelous hazel eyes. Oh," he added quickly, winking
slyly, "you are also the patroness of country songs and
singers."

"I am not joking about this, Peter, so don't you.
Please, I mean it!" She reached out and put her hand
on his arm. "Please," she reechoed, her voice husky.

His grin faded and his lips pressed together in a sober
line as he studied her face with questioning eyes. He
was obviously puzzled, even disturbed by her intensity.
He did not answer for what seemed to her an unending
period. When he finally spoke, his manner was positive
and completely serious. "You are Hensley Travis—the
sister of my best friend—and a beautiful woman."

Her cool fingers tightened their grip on his arm.
"And—and if I were not Allan's sister?"

He cupped her face tenderly. "Then I might never
have known you at all." His eyes widened in a look of
sudden awareness. "That would be such a sad
omission—I won't even consider it!"

Hensley caught her breath in a sliver of sound. This
moment shimmered between them like a mirror-bright
ornament revealing the kaleidoscopic pattern of her
emotions.

Chapter 11

Sleep had not come easily that night. Between Emma's questions and Peter's late visit, Hensley's emotions had been like a Ping-Pong ball bouncing back and forth between too many paddles.

Now, as the persistent brrrrr of the alarm clock awakened her, she stretched and took a few minutes to let the pleasant prospect of going out to Peter's ranch fill her mind with happy thoughts.

Following a brisk shower, she dressed quickly in blue jeans and a red pullover sweater. As she ate a sweet roll and drank some coffee, she recalled some of the things Allan had told her about the Merrick property. "When you first come up over the rise in the road and see it, all spread out diamond-shaped in front of you—the house first and the mountains rising in the distance—you can actually feel it," he had said. "You feel the permanence. You know the house and the land will always be there waiting for you, because the mountains are there standing guard to keep it all secure." She sighed. If only Allan could be going with her today. . . .

She took the last swallow of coffee; she must hurry. It would be cold; she hoped her fisherman's knit sweater-coat would be warm enough. Jamming a navy stocking cap over her hair, she headed out the door.

Peter waited on the front porch, his hand raised in a wave of greeting as Hensley drove up the driveway. Momentarily still, Georgie Girl sat at Peter's feet, her ears erect and her black eyes shining. As soon as

Hensley got out of the car, the dog raced to greet her. Sniffing Hensley's jean-clad legs, Georgie began wagging her tail in friendly approval.

"Hi, there, doggie," she said, bending down to pat the black-and-tan head and rub the animal's sides. "You're nice and friendly. Is this the same dog Allan talked about?" she asked, looking up at Peter.

"This is Georgie Girl, all right. She and Allan were the best of pals. Georgie must somehow associate you with him, because she's not often so pleased with female visitors to the ranch. She reigns as queen here, therefore she's jealous of any woman who enters her domain." Peter laughed and rubbed the dog's neck. Then, with his arm around Hensley's shoulders, they walked away from the car.

"I'm glad Georgie Girl has bestowed her favor on me," she said, smiling.

"Both of us are happy to have you here." He hugged her shoulder.

"Then I'm glad on both counts," she said gaily.

"I have the horses saddled and ready for our ride, Hensley. If it's O.K. with you, we'll go right on down to the barn." Peter was already lengthening his stride, so they were walking faster. "I'm a little leery of our weather prospects, and if we want to have time to ride over all the ranch, we'll have to move along." He kept glancing overhead, and a frown accompanied his words.

"I noticed as I drove out that the sky is gray and looks heavy somehow." She tipped her head back, following his glance.

"Heavy with snow, I'm afraid! Snow is in the forecast for early afternoon, so I think we can have our ride and beat the weather back to the house for lunch." He had released her shoulder and now took her hand, pulling her after him toward the barn. Georgie Girl trotted along close on their heels.

Hensley found Copper Belle to be easy to manage,

just as Peter had promised. She soon felt her initial uneasiness vanish and she rode in relaxed confidence over the rolling terrain of winter brown grass. Copper Belle and Rusty, the roan-colored horse Peter was riding, walked along abreast of each other, making it easy for her and Peter to talk as they rode.

Time passed quickly as Peter pointed out areas of interest, particularly one section of grassy ridges grooved by a coulee. Hensley was fascinated to learn that a coulee was a gulch or ravine.

"Coulee—coulee," she repeated the word, forming a circle with her lips. "Certainly is a pretty name for a gulch," she added, laughing.

They rode ahead for perhaps a quarter of an hour before Peter drew his horse to a halt, and Copper Belle stopped as if guided by the same rein. "This is the most scenic section of our land," Peter said, "and my favorite place. At this point we're at the farthest edge of the ranch. If you visualize the ranch as a diamond," he indicated, drawing the shape in the air with his forefinger, "the house is located at the base point of the diamond, and where we are right now is the top point, the peak."

Hensley leaned forward in the saddle, watching him. "Allan spoke of your place as a diamond to me once, I remember. I understand now exactly what he meant." She looked beyond Peter to the mountains. "It almost seems like we could reach out to the mountains, doesn't it? Those snowy peaks rise so high they must touch the stars." She sighed and shook her head slowly. "I'd like to think it was from this very place that Allan got his feeling for Montana's mountains," she said solemnly.

"It very well could have been, Hensley. He and I rode here dozens of times." Peter's voice was husky; he hesitated, clearing his throat. "We rode out here when he came in April."

"It's so beautiful here—where mountains wait." Her voice trembled. "Allan said the mountains offered the feeling of strength and permanence. The two things he was fighting to have in his life, and he lost them both." She wept silently.

Peter took her horse's bridle, moving the two horses abreast of each other. He covered her hand then with his. "Don't cry, please, Hensley," he said gently. "I don't want you to be sad that you rode here with me. I want everything about your visit to the ranch today to make you feel glad you came!"

"I'm glad I'm here." She blinked at her tears. "I'm not crying because I'm sad, only because I believe I truly understand Allan's feelings for the mountains now. They are beautiful, rocky sentinels towering there to guard the land. Allan would so have loved to belong to all of this as you do, Peter." She turned away and brushed the moisture from her cheeks with the back of her hand.

"Come on," he said suddenly, swinging out of his saddle and jumping to the ground. "Let's forget those tears and walk around under these old pine trees for a while. You'll discover they've dropped such a bed of needles it's like walking on carpet." He reached up to lift her down from her horse, holding her a moment in the air, then slowly letting her body slide through his hands as he lowered her until her feet could touch the ground. He continued to keep his hands at each side of her waist as they stood only inches apart. The masculine smells that clung to him, of tobacco, leather and horses, filled her nostrils. He seemed to get an immense satisfaction out of looking at her and touching her, for he made no move to stop doing either.

"Why is it every time I get my hands on you you're either all wrapped up in a heavy sweater or carrying a huge bundle in front of you?" His eyes now held a teasing smile. "One of these times I'm going to hold you when I can feel the lovely softness I know is hiding under all this protective covering."

She could feel her heart race, and she knew she was

blushing, because his eyes, hands and words aroused her in a way that was new to her.

"I—I've learned to keep my guard up," she said, trying for a witty comeback.

"I'll just bet you have," he snapped, sliding his hands almost roughly down the sides of her body. "I'm certain that working at the motel with your singer friend, you've discovered he doesn't always keep his hands on his guitar strings." Peter's voice was full of rancor, and he underlined the word "motel."

She stared at him as if she were viewing a stranger, and her indignation left her speechless. If he had struck her, she could not have been more taken aback. His lightning change of mood and manner seemed inexplicable.

"I should never have allowed you to take up with that songwriter in the first place," he added sharply.

"Take up—and what connotation are you giving to that?" She flung her head back, eyes blazing.

"I mean, I should have forbidden you to associate with such a cheap opportunist." His tone was arrogant. "Certainly Allan would never have permitted his sister to do it."

"Allan was hardly the pompous tyrant you are, and he did not forbid me to do anything." Anger made her voice uneven. "And let me tell you something, Peter. Allan would not have felt any of the things about Craig that you seem to." She chewed the corner of her lip, determined not to cry and allow Peter the satisfaction of seeing how his ugly insinuations had hurt her. Squaring her shoulders, she looked directly into his face. "Furthermore, I know of nothing which gives you the right to tell me what I am allowed to do. You're not my brother—now it would seem you are not even my friend."

"Damm it, Hensley," he said. "I guess I did come up with a short fuse. I apologize." He reached for her hand, but she jerked it away. "Look . . ." His voice thickened. "I said I was sorry. Isn't that enough?" He made no effort to disguise his belligerence, adding fuel to her anger.

"You're not sorry, Peter." She shook her head at him. "What you are is an overpowering snob. You think you're better than Craig because you have money and position—because you don't need any help and he does." She struggled to get her emotions under control, clenching her fingers in a tight fist to keep them from trembling. "You—You, Peter—you don't need anybody or anything but COPPER." She was furious, and she flung the words at him, revealing the extent of her animosity.

He took a step toward her, catching hold of her, pinning her arms against her sides, caging her in the vise of his embrace. "Do you know you're beautiful—beautiful and exciting." His voice was hoarse with emotion. "And you are quite right about me as well." His eyes sparked with a kind of jubilation, as if she had in some way delighted him with what she had intended to be scathing words. "But don't you see, you're learning to care about copper as much as I do. It's like Allan told you. You belong here, Hensley." He pressed her even closer, and his warm breath brushed her face like a caress. "No country-western singer is going to lure you away from these mountains," he said, and sliding his hand up her back, he curved it around her neck, pulling her lips to his. He kissed her with a fierce deliberateness that brought all of her senses vibrantly alive. The ground seemed to rock beneath her feet and she was falling into a whirlpool of emotions. There was an overpowering magnetism about Peter which seemed to pull her until her body melted against his. As she clung to him, a strange feeling of helplessness caused her heart to flutter like a caged bird, and she could not stop her own betraying responses to the possessive demands of his mouth.

When he finally released her, she was breathless. He

113

looked into her eyes. "You and I should ride here more often," he said. He did not touch her or kiss her again. Instead, he gave her a smile filled with all that consuming charm of his as he said, "Come on, now, pretty girl. We had better start back before the heavens drop their burden of snow on our backs. From the looks of the sky, it wouldn't surprise me a bit if the snow starts before we can reach the barn."

Like turning on and off a light bulb, he had reverted to the Peter she knew. She felt at a loss now to comprehend what all the furor had been about. It almost seemed as if Craig had never been mentioned and that for the past thirty minutes she and Peter had not railed at each other, but had only walked together over a carpet of pine needles and viewed the distant mountains. She did not understand him; she wondered if she ever would. And had he kissed her only to appease her anger? Was it his way of apologizing?

Georgie Girl was waiting when they returned, greeting the two of them with excited barking as she ran back and forth between the two horses. Large flakes of snow were beginning to swirl in the air, sifting gently down and settling like fallen white petals on top of the brown grass.

Peter led Hensley into the high-ceilinged foyer of the house. While he went to the kitchen to inspect the black iron pot of chili he had left simmering on the stove for their lunch, Hensley went upstairs to freshen up from the ride. He urged her to take her time and look around the rooms as much as she liked.

After she had retouched her makeup and combed her hair, she followed his suggestion, making a tour of the multiwindowed sunroom and the four bedrooms. The rooms were not large, but the beamed ceilings and tall casement windows gave them a spacious look. The dark-brown-stained wood of the doors and baseboards emphasized the ivory whiteness of the walls. Hand-woven Indian rugs in rich tones of red, brown and tan covered large areas of the polished wood floors, while the long windows were draped with open-weave casement cloth curtains the color of warm sand.

Entering the largest bedroom at the far end of the hall, she knew immediately that it was Peter's, for the pleasant aroma of his after-shave seemed to hover in the room. She walked over to the table next to the bed and picked up his pipe, which lay beside a can of tobacco. It was the same one she had filled for him when they drove to Butte. Smiling, she thought that someone should warn him it was dangerous to smoke in bed. Absently she rubbed the smooth bowl of the pipe across the palm of her hand, then replaced it on the table. A trade magazine on the copper industry and the current copy of *Newsweek* were neatly stacked next to the reading lamp. She shrugged, thinking of Peter's preoccupation with his business.

Turning away, she noticed the louvered doors to the clothes closet were open. Peter certainly had an orderly array of suits, slacks and sport jackets. Perhaps it was prying, but she felt compelled to look more closely. The sight of the herringbone jacket Peter had worn the Sunday at the copper mine caused her breath to catch in a happy sigh. Remembering the feel of his arms holding her to prevent her from falling caused a sensation like a hundred needle pricks to tingle along her arms. She reached in, touching the jacket, rubbing her hand over the woolen fiber. It had been that same night that Peter kissed her for the first time. She thought again of it now, a good-night kiss, the kind a man like Peter gives the sister of his best friend. Had it been like that? Today he had kissed her for the second time. She closed her eyes, remembering those long, wonderful, breathless minutes. She moved away from the closet, a soft smile of delightful awareness parting her lips. There had been nothing brotherly in Peter's kiss this morning. The rugged mountains could attest to that.

Georgie Girl had followed her upstairs and now lay sprawled contentedly beside a platform rocker in the upstairs sitting room. As she walked through the room, Hensley stopped and bent down to pat the friendly animal's black-and-tan coat. "Ready for a noonday nap, Georgie Girl?" she said, pulling gently on the dog's silky black ears. The dog responded with a lazy wag of her cropped tail. As Hensley walked from the sitting room, she could see through the windows that it was snowing hard now and that the ground below was already carpeted in white.

Hensley descended the curving staircase slowly, trailing her hand along the polished mahogany balustrade. At the foot of the stairs she had just turned to go into the living room when she became aware of voices, apparently coming from a room adjacent to the entrance hall. She walked toward the arched opening into this room, her steps silenced by the hall carpet. The foyer narrowed in a recess before the archway, and she could determine now that the room was a small library. Without definite intention, she hesitated a few feet from the doorway, surprised at hearing a female voice in conversation with Peter.

"Doesn't it seem to you, Peter, that you may be carrying your boy-scout duties a bit far? After three months, I'd say you had already earned your merit badge for care and protection of your young ward!" The woman's words made a sizzling sound, as if they had been spattered on a hot griddle.

"What are you implying by that ridiculous statement, Margo?"

"I'm not *implying* anything at all. I am saying straight out that I do not understand why you find it necessary to plan so many activities for Hensley Travis. You can't really tell me that Allan intended for you to guard her every moment, when he only asked you to look out for her trust money!"

"Margo, for God's sake!" Peter's voice was tight with anger. "Just because I failed to tell you I was showing Hensley around the ranch this morning, must you make a federal case of it?"

"Don't get uptight, darling!" Margo's tone became silken and though she now pitched her voice lower, her words carried easily to Hensley's ears. "I assure you you're taking my meaning in the wrong way," she drawled. "I just felt you should consider the possibility that Hensley could misunderstand all of your constant attentions and kind little acts. You know she could see them as romantic overtures! Don't lose sight of the fact, Peter, that Allan asked you to take care of his sister's financial security—not seduce her!" She spit the last words at him with underscored scarcasm. "By the way, where is your little responsibility?"

"Where is who?" Hensley walked into the library seething with anger. She could feel a pulsing knot in her throat. Drawing a deep breath, she made an instantaneous decision to carry this moment through with cool aplomb, if she could manage to, and then escape as quickly as possible.

Peter spun around at the sound of her words, his eyes revealing acute embarrassment. He appeared to mask it, however, and with a step toward her he said, "I was just telling Margo I'd taken you for your first view of the ranch."

"There's so much to see. We had a wonderful ride." She felt a surge of relief, for her words came evenly and her breathing had resumed a normal pattern.

"I'm sorry I was too late to join you," Margo replied, resting her hand on the back of the leather armchair. "I often ride with Peter on weekends. I shied away today because of the weather predictions." Her voice was now placed deliberately low. She purred her words softly and allowed her fingers to slide gracefully across the smooth leather. Even though her violet eyes held a disarming semismile, Hensley was keenly aware that her attitude was one of cool superiority. Watching Margo's performance made Hensley's blood boil.

"I noticed from the upstairs windows that it's getting to be a real snowstorm outside." Hensley turned her attention to Peter. "I believe I won't hang around to find out," she said lightly. "I hate to miss your good chili, but I feel I should drive back to town before the roads become hazardous. I—I'm sorry, Peter." She took a step toward the door.

"Don't worry about the snow", Peter said putting his hand out to detain her. "I can drive you in later in the pickup if it's really a bad storm."

"No, I must go!" Hensley turned quickly and moved to the doorway. Margo leaned against the chair with an attitude of complete disinterest in this mundane conversation about the weather. Hensley sensed the awkwardness of this entire situation for Peter, although maybe it was mostly her imagination, for he appeared to be handling the problem of two female guests as adeptly as a practiced juggler. Perhaps she was capitulating too readily. After all, she was here at Peter's invitation—but possibly Margo was too. She had said she usually rode with Peter. Hensley chewed the corner of her lip. *Was* Peter only doing his boy-scout act where she was concerned? Was it just a good-turn-daily? Did Peter's attentions to her contain all of the belittling connotations Margo had so archly described? She tensed her shoulders, railing inwardly at the thought. She felt her movements to be gauche as she fumbled in her purse for her car keys, bundled herself into her bulky knit sweater and donned the childish-seeming stocking cap. She felt relieved when she was finally on the front porch with the icy wet air stinging her face. Peter and Georgie Girl were beside her, each acting reluctant to see her go. Peter brushed the snow from her windshield and rear window.

As she slipped behind the steering wheel, Peter touched her arm, holding it briefly. "I'll call you later—I'm sorry things turned out like this—another time, Hensley?" He questioned her with his eyes as well as his voice. "Promise me we'll do this another time soon?"

"I'd like to," she answered, then eased the car down the snow-covered drive. She knew he stood there in the cold watching her car until she was out of sight, for she kept glancing in her rearview mirror. This gave her a nice feeling.

The road from Peter's house rose and dipped before it merged with the main highway. Hensley drove cautiously. The swirling snow now formed a swaying curtain in front of the car. It was like driving in a slow-moving parade through a shower of white confetti. The windshield wipers whished rhythmically as they cleared their fan-shaped arcs.

She wished she could push aside the conversation she had overheard as the wipers did the snow, but she could not. Margo Lawrence had staked a firm claim on Peter's attentions, and who could say she did not have the right? Certainly she and Peter had some kind of understanding between them. Didn't everyone in Anaconda label them a twosome? Ray Holden had said as much—even Emma had implied it. Naturally Margo was not willing to brook interference in her relationship with Peter. Why should she?

Hensley gripped the steering wheel with tense, cold fingers. Flexing her fingers, she relaxed first one hand and then the other. She felt a sudden urge to fling her head back and crow. Why, Margo's behavior was not only understandable, it was predictable. She resented *her man* nursemaiding somebody's little sister because it made her feel threatened!

Hensley relaxed her shoulders, relishing the smug

ripple of warmth her thoughts generated within her. So, Margo Lawrence saw her at least as a slim threat to her hold on Peter. Hensley smiled at this realization, finding it delightful to contemplate.

Chapter 12

Although it was still two weeks until Christmas, Hensley had completed her shopping and had vowed to wrap packages and put up decorations well in advance of the holidays. She had the dining table covered with shiny wrapping paper and rolls of red and green ribbon. Having made multiple loops of red ribbon, she began pulling and separating them to form a large, full bow.

The door buzzer sounded insistently and was immediately followed by a rapid series of loud knocks. "Hey, Hensley—Hey in there!" She heard Craig yell as he kept on pounding the door. "Let me in—I've got something big to tell you!"

"I'm coming," she hollered. "Don't splinter my door!"

Craig burst through the doorway waving a cowboy hat that he instantly sailed across the room. "I just got back from Cheyenne and, baby, did I hit the jackpot! My big chance—it's come, I've really got something going for me. You won't believe what happened!"

"Yes I will, if you'll just draw a deep breath and tell me sanely instead of going off like a bomb exploding," she said, sitting down on the couch and pulling him down beside her. "Now, slowly, one word at a time."

"Hensley, I was lucky enough to get in a real rap session with a song plugger from Sprucewood," he told her, his eyes sparking with excitement. "That's a publishing company in Music Square—the publishing and recording district of Nashville. What I mean is, that's where the action really is. And get this, this guy has set up an audition for me for January fifteenth—a legitimate, bona-fide, in-the-flesh audition! Can you buy that?" He bounced off the couch, tossing his arms over his head and waving his fists in the air like a victorious prizefighter. "Your boy Craig here has got himself one great big chance!"

She laughed at his antics, knowing she had never seen anyone more keyed up than Craig was at this moment.

"Once I get to Nashville I'll be able to promote other auditions. I'll have good, solid opportunities to sell my songs and myself!" He rocked on the heels of his cowboy boots, his body in perpetual motion in his excitement. "It's tough and it's competitive—I know that, but my songs have a hook. The guy from Sprucewood said it. And a hook will catch and hold a listener. My songs touch the feelings of people, and that's what it's all about, Hensley baby!" He pounded his palm with his fist. "I've got to get my hands on a pretty good hunk of money, enough to get me to Nashville and so I can live till I get the breaks. I'll beg, borrow or steal the money some way, 'cause by God I'm going for that audition! Nothing is going to stop me now!"

Hensley shivered, a prickling sensation running along her arms. Craig's avalanche of words seemed to charge the air.

"Hold on for a minute," she said, burying her head in her hands. "Let me try to think about all of this. You know I want to help you"—she lifted her head—"but we'll have to be calm and discover a possible solution." Pursing her lips, she asked, "How much money do you have to have?"

"I'm going to shoot for two thousand dollars. Sounds

like a lot, but I don't know what kind of expenses I could run into. I'll need to make some tapes. Then, if I should cut a demo record, I'd have to pay for a recording studio, sound equipment, and maybe some backup musicians." He shook his head. "Recording songs can run into money," he said, frowning. "Do you reckon you could help me get someone like Mr. Merrick interested in backing me?" Craig's gray eyes narrowed thoughtfully.

"I doubt it," she said. "Peter is not exactly tuned in to country music. His interest is strictly copper."

"O.K. What if we presented him with an angle that would tie into his interest. I'd call myself Copper Reilly—say I hail from copper country USA." He grinned. "I could even dye my hair orange-red, if you think that would help—my beard too. How does that grab you?"

"You have to be joking."

"Nope! I'm willing to do, say or be anything to get the money I need to take me where I have got to go!" The grin had faded from his face and his words were steel-edged. "I don't have your kind of education or connections, classy lady. Hell, all I've got is a guitar and a handful of songs!"

"You have talent," she said quietly. "I will see that you get the money you need."

He stared at her. "Can you? Oh, my God, Hensley, can you really do that?" He stood in front of her, his body rigid as if he dared not move lest she withdraw her offer.

"I have a little money. I'll make arrangements to get it for you. Give me a little time and I'll take care of it." She could hear the tremor in her voice; she felt both nervous and excited. She was not actually too sure she could get as much money as Craig wanted.

"Yipeeeeeeeeeee!" Craig shouted in raucous glee. Grabbing both her hands, he yanked her from the couch and wrapped his arms around her waist in a bear hug of unleashed joy. "Baby, you'll never regret this. I'll pay you back every penny, I promise you."

She felt the warmth of his breath in her hair. He was holding her so close she could scarcely breathe in his tight embrace. He began to nuzzle her neck, still talking to her.

"I never had anything worthwhile in my life until you. That first night you heard my songs, it was fate. Like my lyrics"—his voice was husky pressing against her ear—"my darling, I need you—you know it takes two—to sing my heart-song. It could happen for us, Hensley. We could make it together in Nashville—we could make love and music." His hand curved around the side of her neck, his fingers in her hair as he trailed his lips across her cheek.

As his mouth moved against her lips she pushed against his chest, at the same time pulling back from his embrace. "I think it's best if you remain a free agent for a while," she said, catching her breath. "The offer is tempting"—she smiled—"but you really should concentrate only on your music until you get established on the Nashville scene. I'll stay with the Montana mountains like my brother wanted me to."

He watched her closely, rubbing his bearded chin in a manner that partially shielded his face. "Yeah—I should have expected you would," he answered in a slow drawl. "Like I said, a guy like me is outclassed by the Peter Merricks of this world."

She did not detect any trace of rancor in Craig's tone. If he felt surprise or disappointment at her gentle put-down, he showed no evidence of it.

"You say the darnedest things, Craig. I—I honestly don't know how to take you."

"That's exactly the point, isn't it?" he said. "You don't want to take me at all!"

Hensley frowned, not knowing how to respond to his statement.

A slow grin spread across Craig's face. "It's O.K., classy lady," he said, and moved with an easy swagger to retrieve his hat. "We'll just make music—plenty of good ol' country music."

Peter had been in Denver on business for several days, so Hensley could not talk to him about taking money from her trust for Craig. The morning he returned, she asked Emma to see if Peter could arrange to see her for a few minutes in the afternoon. Emma promised to call her.

As the afternoon passed, Hensley had difficulty concentrating on her work. After several strikeovers, she ripped the sheet she was typing from her typewriter, crumpled it into a ball and aimed it at the wastebasket. In her aggravation she overshot her target. She retrieved the wad of paper, fuming in irritation at herself, and placed it in the center of the scrap-paper-filled container.

Her phone rang. It was Emma, summoning her to Peter's office. She tucked her print blouse smoothly into the waistband of her tailored green skirt and fluffed her hair before she walked into Peter's office.

"You're a pretty sight to brighten the end of a long day," he said, smiling. His complimentary greeting made her glad she had taken those few seconds.

"I appreciate the kind words. It's been one of those days," she added with a laugh.

"Emma tells me you've a problem to discuss with me. How about if we handle it and then I'll charcoal you a steak for dinner at the ranch?" He reached for his pipe.

"Oh, I'd like that!" She felt a warm glow of pleasure at his words.

Peter pulled a chair up close to his desk for her. "Now, what's the problem?" he asked, rolling his swivel chair closer to her.

"I need some money from the trust." She swung one

leg over the other and thus matched his appearance of relaxed composure for their conversation.

"Well, now, if your allowance is feeling the pressure of your Christmas shopping, I think a little bonus for this month is entirely in order. How much do you need, fifty—a hundred?" His voice was warm and teasing. She had the fleeting impression that he was indulging her as one would a pampered child. Knowing the thought was unworthy, she pushed it aside.

"It's not Christmas shopping, Peter. I need two thousand dollars, possibly even twenty-five hundred."

Peter jerked upright in his chair. The abrupt movement caused his chair to swivel a quarter turn. He grabbed hold of the desk to steady himself. "My God, Hensley," he said loudly. "What on earth could you possibly need twenty-five hundred dollars for? Surely you're not considering trading in your car on a new model?"

"No, of course not." She laughed. "It's not that I want to buy anything. I'm lending the money to Craig Reilly."

"You want to lend that singer a sum like that?" Peter's tone was incredulous.

"Craig has a tremendous opportunity. He's to go to Nashville for an audition and to get some of his songs recorded. I want to help him."

"The *hell* you do!" Peter slammed his desk with the flat of his hand. "That's idiotic!"

She stared at Peter coldly. "I don't see anything idiotic about it. If I wish to help Craig with my own money I believe I have the right to do so." She spoke the words evenly. "It is *my* trust money," she stated positively, folding her hands tightly together in her lap. Peter's yelling irritated her, but she was determined to stay cool.

"Look here, I'm sorry for my outburst—I shouldn't have come on so strong." He rubbed his forehead. "Let me explain some pertinent facts to you," he said, modulating his tone of voice. "You already get most of the income from the trust in your monthly allowance. For you to obtain a sum like you're talking about, we'd have to sell one of your investments," he said, focusing his steady gaze on Hensley's resolute face. "You can't liquidate assets for a foolish venture that has no guarantee of any return. It's damn poor business, and as trustee, I cannot allow it!"

"Frankly, I don't care about what is good business and what isn't!" She resented his attempt to trap her with his logic and reason. "Don't preach economics to me, either. It is quite annoying. I insist you sell something and get the money for me. I want two thousand dollars." She folded her arms across her breast, intending the gesture to indicate that she considered the matter closed.

"Hensley, you're not listening. Even if I wanted to, I *cannot* do it! The trust is set up so it cannot be tampered with. The only exception is if the money were needed for your own personal health or general welfare. There are no allowances made for you to indulge some romantic whim because you've gotten involved with a singing cowhand!" Peter now made no attempt to disguise his exasperation with her.

"Involved . . ." She found his words and attitude infuriating. "Involved . . ." she repeated, lashing his word back at him. "Are you still conjuring up some picture of me as Craig Reilly's woman? Is that how you see me?" She flung questions in bitter anger.

"Is it how you see yourself?" His tone was pure vitriol.

"*No!* Of course I do not. But I do find it pleasant to know a man who does not treat me like an overindulged child for a change. At least Craig sees me as a woman—one he needs and wants!"

"You bet he does! That aggressive opportunist needs your charm, your social acceptance and certainly your money. He's using you, surely you can see that? He'll

126

use you and any other woman he can to further his career!"

"What a despicable thing to say to me. You know very well it's his music I'm interested in. Why do you make it seem like I'm paying for an affair set to country music?" Her voice shook with rage.

"Now, Hensley, let's not argue. We'll put all of this behind us. I'm sure nothing good can come from your getting further involved with this man."

Peter's manner added fuel to her anger. She saw his attempt to cajole her into accepting his judgment as the ultimate insult to her intelligence.

"Stop patronizing me as if I were some simpleminded child!" Her voice was brittle as ice and equally as cold. "Since you will not allow me to have my own money from my own trust, I will get it from another source. I've promised Craig I'll help him, and I'll keep my word. Nothing is going to stop me!" She stood up, holding her back stiff, her head high in defiance. She pushed her hair from her face with a flip of her hand as she said, "I'll get the money from David Gillette. I know *he* will be glad to give it to me."

Pushing back his chair, Peter took a step toward her. "You can bet your sweet life he will. Hell! He'd like nothing better than to have you in his debt. And don't think for a minute he wouldn't use it to his own advantage!"

"I don't believe you, Peter," she sputtered. "What nasty insinuations are you making now about David?"

"When I was in Ironville it was clearly obvious that your boss wanted to control your life for himself. That is more than an insinuation. It's a fact. Furthermore, I think you damn well know it is too, despite the look of girlish innocence you're wearing."

She stared at him. There was an underlying quality in Peter's words she had not heard before. A thought flashed through her mind. Could it be possible Peter was jealous? She felt a shiver of exhilaration. He had been so high-handed with her about the money for Craig that she would welcome any retaliation. The moment of elation faded. It couldn't be jealousy; he was only attempting to force her to comply with his decisions. If he could make her feel immature, she would give up her scheme to aid Craig. These must be the motives behind his angry accusations.

"I dont know why I bother to explain, but I will. I'm not *taking* money from David. I will, however, sell him a pair of Canadian stamps he has been anxious to purchase from my father's collection. You can control my trust fund, Peter, but you cannot prevent me from selling the stamps in order to raise the money I need for Craig." Turning her back, she started toward the door. Tears of frustration and anger, which she had been fighting, now spilled down her cheeks. She quickly tried to wipe them away with trembling fingers.

"Hensley, please, don't go. I want to say—"

"You've had your say." She spun around to face him. "You've made it abundantly clear that in your opinion I'm quite a swinger. The minute my brother dies, I carry on an affair with an older, married man. When that palls, I rush out West to find myself a guitar-playing opportunist to squander my inheritance on. My, my, Peter." She smiled sardonically. "You must agree, it's quite a track record for only six months."

In two long strides he covered the distance between them, grabbing her, shaking her angrily, his fingers squeezing the tender flesh of her shoulders.

She winced, uttering a shrill cry of pain.

"Damn . . . damn you, Hensley Travis!" Peter's face blanched with fury as he swore at her through clenched teeth. "You'd drive a saint to hell—and by God, I'm sure as hell no saint!" Uncontrolled emotion burned in the depths of his eyes as he crushed her body to him and kissed her with ferocious intensity.

She struggled to free herself, pounding him with her fists until the unleashed passion of his mouth consumed her, sending all of her senses reeling. The effect of his nearness and the intimacy of his hands made her heart pound like an explosion inside of her. She was conscious of the warmth and strength of Peter's hands moving over her shoulders and along her arms. It was as if the thin material of her blouse did not exist between her sensitive skin and his caressing touch. He continued to touch her with a lingering gentleness, sliding his hands along the sides of her breasts, circling her waist and finally molding her body to the length of his. She was now aware that the thunder in her ears was not only her own heart but the pounding of Peter's as well, and putting her arms around his neck, she clung to him, her fingers brushing the back of his sandy hair. With her complete acquiescence, Peter's mouth changed, becoming gentle on hers, causing an exquisite warmth to stroke her like a summer breeze.

"I'm sorry about this." Peter's voice was husky. "I don't want to fight with you."

For a second she couldn't help but wonder if he had only been attempting to kiss her into submitting to his way of thinking. She pulled back from him so she could see his face. He gently fingered a stray wisp of her hair, pushing it away from her forehead. She smiled up at him, finding his caring gesture disarming.

"I don't want to fight either," she said softly. "And I do understand your position about the trust, Peter. I even realize why you can't allow me to have money from it, but"—she squared her shoulders—"I'm not changing my mind. I *am* going to sell the stamps and give Craig the money I promised."

"I know you are. You're so damned determined about this song business!" She could see his mouth firmly pressed in that set way of his, but there was a glint of a smile in his dark eyes as he added, "I should have learned by now I can't put a bridle on an impulsive filly like you." He pulled her back again into his arms.

"I guess you're finding doing a good turn daily for an

unreasonable girl is rather a thankless chore," she said softly, her lips almost touching his.

"You did hear that ridiculous hogwash of Margo's, didn't you?" he said, kissing her lips gently, then smoothing the frown line between her eyes with his finger.

She nodded. "I even understand it. If I knew you in the way Margo does, I'd take the very same attitude she has." She allowed a wistful tone to color her words.

Peter studied her expression, his face marked by surprise. "You're still an enigma to me, you know that?" He smiled. "And too damned provocative for office hours!" He released her slowly. "Now, get out of here so I can finish my work." He grinned and gave her a little shove.

She walked by Emma's desk, giving her a smile, but not stopping to talk. She didn't want to talk to anyone now. All she really wanted was to remember the feel of Peter's arms holding her and his mouth kissing her in such a thoroughly satisfying way. Had he felt some of the same emotions she had? Surely he had? Surely he cared for her? She felt a tinge of elation. At least he no longer saw her as a *little girl*. She felt quite positive of that!

Chapter 13

An hour later, as Hensley drove along the snow-banked streets toward her apartment, she noticed how beautiful everything looked clothed in December's white garb. It could be her joyous mood that was making her aware of every detail of the winter scene, but truly the snowfall of the past few days had robed the stately pine trees so that they appeared like groups of silent angels awaiting the holy celebration of Christmas. She had not actually looked forward to Christmas before this afternoon. She had to admit she had feared the loneliness this holiday can bring when you are alone and without family. Now she had a heady sense of expectancy that exhilarated her. "Whoa—slow down," she said aloud, and then laughed to herself because she had spontaneously braked the car. Her verbal cautioning had not of course concerned her driving but had been aimed at her overexuberance. In the past, Allan had been the one to admonish her about this trait of hers. At this moment she knew nothing could diminish her high spirits, for she could not feel the way she did about Peter unless he felt something like it too—could she?

She pulled into her parking slot and locked the car. Crossing the courtyard, she stopped by the row of mailboxes at the foot of the stairs to pick up her mail. There appeared to be a handful of Christmas cards, some sporting holiday red and green envelopes. At the top of the stairs she paused to admire the green fir wreath that enhanced her door. She was glad she had bought this one, with its huge red bow of vinyl ribbon; it looked so festive, and the ribbon made a crackling sound of greeting, for it had been starched by the icy air.

Unlocking the door, she entered and immediately turned on a table lamp, which made a circle of yellow light in the dusky room. Though it was just past five o'clock it was already growing dark outside; the whiteness of the snow-covered ground made the purple twilight seem dark in contrast. Adjusting the thermostat to increase the flow of heat, she hung her coat up and walked into the kitchen to check the exact time on the electric clock above the stove. She wondered if there was a possibility that she could catch David at the newspaper. Although it was another, later time zone in

Minnesota, she knew David was in the habit of staying after work much of the time. She would try to reach him at the *Journal*.

"David? It's Hensley! I thought I might catch you still hard at work on tomorrow's edition. Merry Christmas!"

"God, Hensley!" his voice boomed. "Merry Christmas to you, and it's great hearing your voice. How are you, anyway?"

"I'm super, David. It's white and beautiful here, but awfully cold. How's everything in Ironville?"

"There's no heat wave here—you remember Minnesota in December! Let's skip the weather, what's on your mind, honey?"

She laughed. It was so like David to be blunt. She well remembered that he never was one to want to beat around the bush about anything. "I called to ask if you might still be interested in that Cartier stamp in Dad's collection." She paused. "I seem to be in need of a little money," she added with an embarrassed laugh. "I'd really like to sell you that pair of stamps."

"I sure as hell am interested; you know how I've coveted those stamps! Say, have you put the collection up for sale?" he asked eagerly.

"No, nothing like that; I just need to sell this one pair." With a rising inflection in her voice she asked, "David, you're not interested in any of the other stamps anyway, are you?"

"Right, it's only the Cartier that I need for my set, but it's a funny coincidence. A stamp dealer in Duluth contacted me about a month ago. It seems a couple of pairs of that Canadian series have been on the market. I wondered at the time if it could possibly be from your father's collection. As far as I know, your Dad's set was the only one in this area." He raised his voice and began speaking faster. "Do you recall the rose-colored Victoria stamp and the red lilac Prince Albert? Those were the two pairs being offered."

132

Hensley interrupted David's excited words detailing the stamps. "That's all most interesting, David, but you know I'm a washout as a stamp buff."

"I even asked point-blank if it was the Travis collection he was selling." David took up the conversation, ignoring her statements. "Those damn dealers—they're all vague and secretive when it comes to their sources. This dealer has a reputable background or else I'd have thought he was fencing stolen stamps, he was so evasive with me!" David's voice had assumed roaring proportions. Hensley held the receiver away from her ear.

"I just can't get as worked up as you do about a piece of colored paper an inch square! Anyway, hold on and we'll discuss stamps when I get to Ironville. How about if I fly to Duluth the day after Christmas? If I can make good connections, I'll catch a short shuttle flight to Ironville or rent a car at the airport and drive from Duluth."

"Fine! Just plan to stay a few days! I mean it, Hensley; I won't take no on that, so you just plan right now to capitulate to my wishes on that score!"

"Don't be so bossy." She laughed. "I will stay two or three days. I'll need to get the stamps from the bank, and I should close out that deposit box. David, I do appreciate it."

"Forget it! You're the one who's doing me a favor. Remember, I told you the first time I ever saw you that I wanted to own that Jacques Cartier pair!" She instantly pictured that spring day in her mind. She could just see David, wagging his glasses at her as he talked. She would bet he was sitting at his desk just the same way right now, his glasses in his hand and his blue eyes beaming out from under sandy red brows.

As she hung up the telephone, she looked at her watch. It was getting late; if she wanted to shower and be in her new coral dress by the time Peter arrived to take her to the ranch, she had better hurry.

Peter took one look at her when she held the door open for him and gave out a slow whistle of approval. "That's quite a change from your sedate office attire," he said, eyeing the plunging neckline of her coral-red gown. "Ummm—quite something." He raised one dark eyebrow.

Hensley made a pirouette, causing the soft folds of jersey to swirl out, then settle back and cling softly to the curves of her body. "I'm glad you like it; it's my Christmas present to myself."

"I like it, all right." He grinned. "Makes me think of a day years ago when little Hensley Travis peered at me through big sunglasses in a teenage attempt to appear sophisticated. Well, I have to tell you, you've got it made in that outfit. You not only look sophisticated, but sexy as well. If I were wise, I'd turn and run like hell." With a backward step toward the door, he made a motion as if to leave.

"You're making fun of me as if I were still a thirteen-year-old." She shook her finger at him and frowned. "And believe me, Peter, if I knew a way to get back at you, I would. Here I spend a bundle on this dress to change my little-sister image, and all you do is belittle my efforts."

"Believe me, honey, your efforts were not in vain. I'm not belittling; I'm simply fighting my natural impulses." He made a playful grab at her.

Ducking out of his reach, she picked up her coat. "Come on, Peter." She laughed. "I'm getting you out of here and into the cold night air." Taking hold of his hand, she pulled him after her and they left the apartment.

"I stopped to pick up the steaks on my way to get you," Peter explained as they drove toward the ranch. "That's one of the reasons I was delayed. I had to buy some tinsel too, so you could help me decorate the Christmas tree tonight. You won't mind, will you? I've got to do the tree; the Christmas Eve party is only three days from now."

"I'd love to; it'll be fun," she agreed. Emma had told her about the annual open house Peter held for the company on Christmas Eve. It evidently was a tradition started years ago by Peter's father.

Hensley wondered if Peter usually asked Margo to help him with the tree and preparations for the party. She enjoyed a second of malicious glee in the thought that this year she might have scored this coup against Margo. Glancing at Peter's profile, she drew in her breath. Emma's admonition, that she should consider how she might feel if Peter were to marry Margo, surfaced suddenly in her thoughts. She stared at him in startling awareness of the depth of her feelings.

Peter took one hand from the steering wheel and handed her his pipe and tobacco. "You're my pipe expert," he said. "Fill this for me while I drive, will you?" He appeared oblivious of her emotional scrutiny, and she was grateful to be occupied with his pipe. She hoped Peter would not look at her for fear her face would reveal what she was feeling.

They were now out of the city. The snowplows had cleared the highway, leaving a wide black path bordered by four-foot banks of snow. The absence of other cars on the road added to the silent quality of the winter night. All of this intensified the intimate warmth inside the car.

"What about food?" she asked, handing him his pipe. She edged closer to the door and kept her head down, glad that the dimly lit interior of the car shielded her.

"I'll charcoal the steaks as soon as we get to the ranch. I have no intention of starving a lady on a cold night, even though it may seem that way."

"I didn't mean tonight, Peter." She shook her head. "I meant the food for the party."

"Oh." He laughed. "I did think you weren't paying much attention to me. Especially since I had mentioned getting the steaks for tonight at least twice. As for the party, Emma fortunately handles all of that with a catering service." Turning his head, he looked at her, and his voice took on a serious note. "I think you will be interested, however, in one arrangement I did make for the party after you left the office this afternoon."

"Don't tell me you rented a Santa Claus costume?" she said, teasing him.

"Of course not," he scoffed. "I hired Craig Reilly to entertain at the party."

She leaned toward him, her face beaming. "Oh, Peter," she cried, placing her hand on his arm. "That's so good of you. He needs the money, and . . . well, you know, I appreciate your doing this for him."

He covered her hand with his. "I have to confess there was no benevolence in my act. I did it purely and simply to get back in your good graces."

"Well, you succeeded!" She smiled and moved closer to him.

When they arrived at the ranch, Peter promptly got the charcoal started in the outdoor grill. He told Hensley to take whatever looked appetizing from the freezer. She was frankly amazed to discover such a well-ordered supply of frozen foods. She took out a plastic bag containing ears of sweet corn and also a loaf of French bread. Peter took a wooden salad bowl from a cupboard and set it on the kitchen counter. Beside it he placed a head of lettuce, two tomatoes and an avocado. Hensley washed her hands and began tearing lettuce leaves for salad. Peter banged in and out of the kitchen as he tended the grill on the patio.

"A winter night with snow on the ground, and you're cooking steaks out-of-doors. Seems like madness, Peter," she called to him as he barged out the door, steaks in hand.

"Don't call me mad, honey." He grinned. "I'm merely working on my image as an eccentric bachelor!"

"I'd say you had that image well-worked-out already. You've got such a well-stocked larder here, you must be in the habit of entertaining a harem." She arched an eyebrow and peered at him in conjecture.

"Not quite," he said, and winked broadly. "I find I am at my best on a one-to-one basis!"

She shook a tomato at him and grinned.

After dinner they carried their coffee into the living room. Peter had the green Christmas tree in place in front of the windows at the front of the house. Several strands of lights already circled the huge Scotch pine, and open boxes of ornaments were on the floor at the base of the tree, waiting to be hung on the thick branches.

"There have to be fifteen dozen ornaments here," Hensley said, pointing at the boxes. "No wonder you wanted help."

Setting to work, she began hanging glistening red balls along the lower branches while Peter reached for those shoulder height and above. It required a good deal of time and much circling about and eyeing from all sides before they had the tree symmetrically laden with green and red Christmas balls.

"We've accomplished total perfection," she said with a happy sigh.

"Almost!" Peter was untying the only remaining box. He lifted out a metal star from a nest of flannel cloth. "A Merrick heirloom for the top of the tree," he said, holding it up for her to see.

"Oh, Peter, it's made of copper, isn't it?" she exclaimed.

"Yes, it was cut from sheets of copper, and the design on it was crafted by a Zuni Indian friend of my father's. It dates back before I was born, so I've never known a

Christmas without it on our tree." He rubbed the metal with the soft cloth to polish it.

She could sense the pride he felt. "It's lovely, Peter," she said quietly. "I think I envy you such a family tradition."

She watched Peter pull a straight-back chair over to the tree to climb on. Centering the copper star, he secured it to the top of the tree, then swung himself down, pushing the chair back in place against the wall. Turning on the tree lights, he switched off the other lights in the living room. The tree stood majestically in the now darkened room, shimmering in its array of colored lights.

Peter put his arm around her waist so that they stood with their bodies touching as they looked at the tree. "You don't ever need to envy any traditions here, just share them with me."

His words and the tone of his voice moved her unutterably. "Sharing the tree tonight, my first Montana Christmas tree, makes me happy and sad at the same time." Her voice trembled with emotion. "Like hearing a bittersweet melody, it makes me want to cry." She covered her mouth with her hands, holding back her tears.

"You're thinking about Allan," Peter said quietly. "I am too."

"It's almost as if he were here. Don't you feel that, Peter?"

"He would be happy knowing you and I are here together. I'm certain of that," he answered, kissing her silky hair where it lay against her temple. With his arm around her shoulders, they moved across the room and Peter pulled her gently down on the sofa, easing her shoulders back until she was lying against the soft cushions. He seemed to contemplate her face. "I do believe those hazel eyes of yours have cast a spell over me." His voice was gently teasing, but there was a slumberous emotion coming alive in his dark eyes. He let his face brush her cheek, his mouth warm against her hair. "You're a beautiful, desirable woman, Hensley. I've tried to deny that fact, but I can't deny it any longer." He pushed aside the neckline of her coral dress, allowing his hand to slide slowly down the slender column of her neck and move warmly over her bare shoulder. He kissed the hollow of her throat, and as his lips sought the deep, soft valley between her breasts, she could feel her blood run like fire along her veins.

"Peter . . . Peter . . ." She repeated his name in a barely audible sigh.

He lifted his face and she could see the shaft of desire in his eyes. "I've waited so long for you," he said huskily. Brushing her hair away from her cheeks, he began to cover her face with kisses. Then his mouth found hers and he was holding her, caressing her, kissing her as her heart pounded in her breast and echoed with a rushing sound in her ears. Joyously she wound her arms around him, feeling the strong corded muscles that ran down his back, aware too that his heart was beating as hard and fast as her own. The passion of Peter's mouth possessed hers with a sensuality that drew an answering response from her, while the touch of his hands, intimately knowing, embraced her senses with a new and encompassing rapture. It seemed that her body, her mind and her heart were touched in a hundred different ways and the storm of her own clamouring emotions was sweeping her along on a tide of sensations that hovered on the brink of desire. There was an indisputable awareness deep inside her—rich, warm and complete. She was in love with Peter Merrick. She had never felt this way about a man before, not only loving him but wanting him too. She began to tremble—half in anticipation and half in fear of where this was leading. Pushing against his chest, she freed her lips from his. "Peter?" She breathed his name in a questioning whisper. "I . . . I want us to talk. I . . . I need to understand what is happening to me."

He held her face between his hands, looking at her intently. His breathing was uneven, and embers of emotion smoldered in his dark eyes. "I can't say what is happening to you, Hensley. That is for you to decide." A frown knitted his brows. He straightened, shifting his position so he was sitting beside her without their bodies touching. "I can tell you, however, what has already happened to me." He took a deep breath and let it out slowly. "I began to realize the morning we rode together here at the ranch that you belonged here with me." He kept his eyes on her face as he spoke, and the rough edge was gone from his voice. "I have a sense of the land and of this house. When you walked in and I watched you climb the stairs that day, your hand touching the balustrade, it was almost as if I'd seen you there before and watched you go upstairs many times, trailing your hand on the rail in exactly that same way. I was struck with the rightness of it—the rightness of you, Hensley." He hesitated. "I'm not saying this well, am I?"

"You're saying what I want very much to hear. Riding that morning, especially at the far end of your ranch, when we seemed so close to the mountains, I felt secure for the first time since Allan died. Maybe it sounds strange, but there, looking at the mountains, I think I felt what you mean—the rightness, the sense of belonging." Her lips trembled. "But . . ." She pressed her hand to her mouth, turning her head away from Peter.

"But what?" He frowned.

"Well, later, with Margo, I felt awkward. I was the intruder somehow, and nothing felt right for me then." She kept her eyes averted and pushed herself into a sitting position on the sofa.

"I hated it to happen like it did." He crossed the room to the fireplace as he spoke. Picking up the poker, he jabbed at the red embers. "Perhaps this is the right time to tell you about Margo." His back was to her as he bent over, placing a fresh log on the fire.

Hensley stared at his broad shoulders, feeling suddenly chilled, as if his standing in front of the fire blocked all heat from touching her. What had happened to the warm intimacy they had shared only a moment ago? Why had she allowed Margo to creep into their conversation? She must stop Peter, she thought, for suddenly she felt afraid of what he might say.

"It was the year before my father died that I began seeing a good deal of Margo," he said, turning around and standing with his back to the fire. He kept his hands clasped behind him. "I wasn't prepared to take over as head of the company, but after Dad was gone, of course the job fell to me. I was determined to prevent any break in continuity, and to maintain the degree of success the business had enjoyed under Dad's leadership. The job consumed me."

He did not look directly at Hensley. Instead he seemed to gaze at the lighted tree across the room. "I remember that winter, Allan came out for a week's visit. He met Margo, and the three of us went to Big Sky for the weekend to ski. It was the first weekend I'd spent away from Anoconda in the ten months since my father's death."

" 'Copper is your mistress,'—those were the very words Allan had said to me then. I can hear him now. 'There's no room in your life for another love, not now—only copper. Not even Margo will alter that fact,' he had said."

Peter looked at Hensley now. "Your brother was entirely right. Copper was the one thing most important to me. Merrick Company flourished and I flourished with it. As for Margo, she accepted—even chose, I think—the nondemanding relationship we drifted into."

"Why are you telling me all of this?"

"Because I think it explains why Margo reacted as she did at finding you at the ranch. She sensed the beginnings of a change. You see, she was the first one of us to recognize that Allan had altered the pattern of all our lives."

"Allan?" she questioned in complete surprise.

Peter crossed to the sofa and, sitting down beside her, took hold of her hand. "Your brother understood you, as well as any man could understand an impulsive girl, and he understood me, I do believe, better than I understand myself." Peter's voice was full of warm affection. "Did he ever say anything to you about his wish to leave his mark on something or someone?"

She was puzzled by Peter's words; his recalling Allan this way was suddenly painful to her. She closed her eyes against the poignant memories his words recalled.

"Hensley, don't you see? Allan found the ideal way to do this. He brought the two people he loved together—you and me."

She sighed. "He's influenced us both, of course he has. But, Peter, Allan wasn't trying to play God. You're wrong if you believe that!"

"I'm making a mess of this, saying it all wrong," he said. She could see his frown darken the bright look that had been in his eyes.

"Come with me." He pulled her quickly to her feet. "I've something for you. Something I believe will show you what I've been trying to put into words."

He led her through the hall to the library. As he walked around the end of the desk and opened the drawer, Hensley leaned against the desk, watching him with open curiosity. What could he be up to? she wondered.

In the past hour her spirits had been up and down like a yo-yo. One minute she had been in Peter's arms sublimely happy. Then, just as he had begun to speak caring words to her, she had done or said something that led him to talk of Margo. Why, hadn't he even made explanations for Margo's feelings and actions? It ought to be her feelings, not Margo's, Peter should be concerned about. If he really cared about her, that is.

Her head was beginning to ache. This evening, which had started out so perfectly, now seemed to be teeming with mistakes. Was falling in love with Peter going to prove to be the most painful mistake of all? She swayed, feeling as if she were losing her balance. Putting her hand down on the top of the desk to steady herself, she touched the ebony base on which the piece of copper ore was mounted.

"Why," she exclaimed in surprise, "you brought your father's paperweight home from your office." She picked it up, turning it to examine the various angles of the copper nugget, glad of the distraction from her introspective thoughts.

"Ummm, yeah, I'll take it back tomorrow. I had need of it for a few weeks." He closed the lower drawer of his desk, and with a smile crinkling his eyes, he handed her a small package wrapped in lustrous white paper and centered with an impressive gold medallion sticker in lieu of a ribbon bow.

"Merry Christmas, darling," he said.

Hensley caught her breath. Peter's voice, though pitched low, resounded in the small book-lined room. He had never called her darling before. The endearment echoed its cherished sound in her ears. Her fingers closing around the package trembled with her excitement.

"Please, don't make me wait until Christmas to open this," she pleaded. "I'll surely die of curiosity!"

"I want you to open it now. I want to see if you like

it." He watched as she tore away the shiny paper, uncovering a velvet-covered jeweler's box.

She was acutely conscious of the feel of the soft covering. She lifted the lid and gazed at the copper disk suspended from a hand-crafted copper chain. "Peter . . . Oh, Peter!" She touched the center of the disk where a small nugget of copper was mounted in a pronged setting. "Where did you ever discover an artist who could craft this so perfectly—the metal, with this piece of actual ore . . . Oh . . . *oh!*" It struck her all at once exactly how the pendant had been conceived.

"Merrick copper. It is, isn't it? It's from your piece of the first Merrick ore!" Even looking at it, holding it, she still found it incredible. "Peter, you didn't . . . You didn't really?"

"Yes, I really did!" There was happiness in his eyes and laughter in his voice. He obviously loved every nuance of her pleasure at his gift. "That's the reason the paperweight is still here," he said, smiling broadly. "I just got it, and the finished pendant, back yesterday from the jeweler in Great Falls."

Throwing her arms around him, she buried her face against his neck. "I don't know what to say, I really don't. I can't believe you'd do this for any girl!"

"Not for any girl—but for you, Hensley—for you, who belongs here in these mountains, and who learned from a mining-engineer brother exactly how much the ore can mean to men who make it their life's work." He hugged her, adding, "That is what I've been trying to tell you tonight." He pushed her gently away. "Hey, you're getting my neck wet."

"I can't help it," she said, rubbing her eyes with the back of her hand. "You say all those things to me and I have to cry, because you make me happy."

"Then smile, pretty girl, and make me happy." He moved behind her, fastening the necklace around her neck. Then, holding her shoulders, he pulled her back so she leaned against him. "Allan was wrong, you know." His voice was suddenly husky and his fingers gripped her shoulders. "Copper is not the mistress I want—you are." He kissed the nape of her neck, and the touch of his breath against her bare skin caused her heart to beat raggedly.

She could not move away; indeed, she had no desire to. Touching the copper disk, she felt the throbbing in the hollow of her throat.

Peter turned her into his arms. "Do you have any idea how much I want you?" His rugged, handsome face was bending to hers. "You belong here, Hensley. Stay with me." He held her close, her rounded breasts crushed against the hardness of his chest.

As if she were falling into a whirlpool, she felt a strange helplessness, and she clung to him. Closing her eyes, she struggled with her feelings, her body and mind now in conflict. There could be no doubt that Peter found her beautiful and desirable, but did he love her? He had never said he did. There was the necklace he had given her—a piece of Merrick copper. Would he have done this unless he truly cared for her? But if he loved her, wouldn't he tell her so?

"Darling," he entreated, and there was no denying the question in his voice.

"I . . . I can't," she murmured, burying her face against his neck, knowing she dared not look at him or her resistance would vanish.

For a long moment, neither of them moved. When Hensley finally stirred in his arms, he stepped back, releasing her. "I'll get your coat, drive you back," he said, and there was no readable inflection in his voice.

Outside, Peter opened the car door for her, then walked around to slide in behind the wheel. Hensley kept her eyes fixed on the living-room window, through which was revealed the decorated Christmas tree adorned with its multitude of glowing lights.

Chapter 14

A festive holiday spirit encompassed the party. Sounds of laughter made crescendos from one group of people to the next all around the living room. Hensley stood by the fireplace talking to Ray Holden and two of his friends from the accounting department. She sipped a cup of egg nog, and though she pretended to be paying close attention to Ray's joke-filled banter, she was actually watching Peter over the edge of her raised cup. Peter moved about, mingling with his guests, obviously enjoying his role as host. A blast of laughter from the men around her alerted her attention, and she aimed a bright smile at Ray.

"Well, that's better. I must say, Hensley, for a minute there I thought my witty repartee had fallen on deaf ears!"

"Ray, you're always the life of the party, you know that!" she countered glibly. "You've a captive audience, but excuse me for a minute. I want to ask Craig to play a couple of his new songs for you to hear." Placing her egg nog on the mantel, she heard Ray toss off a parting remark. "You hear that, fellows? I'll have to get myself a guitar if I want to woo this gal. Lately, she's become addicted to that country boy and his *gee*tar music!" He made a woeful grimace.

Hensley made her exit from the living room. She had left her coat and purse upstairs in one of the bedrooms, and she wanted to get the Christmas present she had brought for Peter and slip it into the library where he'd find it later. She was just descending the stairs with the package in her hand when the front door opened and Margo Lawrence came in with two men and a petite auburn-haired girl Hensley had never seen before. They were not people from the company, she knew that much, so undoubtedly they were Anaconda friends of Peter's. They exchanged a flurry of brief greetings, and Hensley turned toward the library as the two women headed up the stairs to leave their wraps. Hensley felt a twinge of resentment at seeing Margo here at Peter's again. She tossed her head in a gesture of irritation, thinking she could not recall being jealous of another person before, but then, there had never been a man like Peter in her life before, either. Her breath caught in a sigh; she put her hand to her breast as if to steady the sudden rapid beating of her heart. Her newly discovered love for Peter absorbed her every emotion as completely as a new sponge assimilates water. Closing her eyes, she fervently wished she could block out all thoughts of any relation that might have existed between Peter and Margo.

With her back to the doorway, she placed the gift for Peter in the center of his desk.

"I'll add my gift to yours." Margo's silky tones startled Hensley. She spun around; the sudden intake of her breath almost choked her.

"You surprised me," she said, coughing to clear her throat.

"I'm sorry," Margo said as she placed a gaily wrapped package on the desk atop the smaller one of Hensley's. With a conspiratorial smile she said, "I'm glad I found you here alone. I really have wanted to talk to you ever since we were both here the morning it was snowing." She wrapped her words in a cocoon of smiles. "It's actually Peter I wanted to talk to you about. I'm going to be perfectly candid." Her smile was disarming. "I do believe I may be a bit jealous of you."

Hensley stared, astounded by Margo's directness. It made her more than a little uneasy to be here listening

147

to a confession of envy coming from Margo's perfectly shaped lips. It was so out of character for this self-assured woman that Hensley had the feeling that it was more of an artful performance designed to accomplish some specific end known only to the actress herself.

Before Hensley could rally her thoughts and reply, Margo continued in another smooth flow of words, "You know, Hensley, Peter and I have been friends for quite a long time. To be utterly frank, until your brother drew Peter into his series of plans concerning you, I had exclusive call on both Peter's time and his affection." Margo's voice now rang with self-confidence, leaving Hensley to feel like a piece of excess baggage for which no one desires to present a claim check.

"Allan and Peter were best friends, and Allan was terminally ill," Hensley responded in an attempt to muster up a dignified rebuttal to Margo's allegations. "Naturally Peter would take time from his other commitments to aid my brother in making financial arrangements for me. This hardly constitutes an infringement on your association with him!"

Margo shrugged. "The ramifications seem to have done just that. Peter does have a boy-scout zest for carrying out duties and obligations, don't you agree?" Her carefully shaped eyebrows arched disdainfully.

"I fail to see the connection," Hensley said evenly, at the same time narrowing her eyes in irritation. "Why does the good-turn connotation of a scout seem to be such a part of your speech?" She kept her words deliberately steady, but anger sparked her voice. "I seem to recall this same utterance from you once before."

"Well, I'll change my figure of speech, if you find it offensive. Let me put it another way. In the performance of his acts as guardian, Peter seems to mistakenly believe he must offer you affection as well as protective concern."

The words slapped Hensley like the lash of a brutal whip. She spun around and took a step away from Margo, staring with unseeing eyes at the book-lined wall of the library.

"This is understandable, of course," Margo continued, voicing her convictions. "His compulsive loyalty to your brother, and his almost holy dedication to carry out the wishes of a dead man, have colored Peter's thinking. When he regains the proper perspective, and I'm certain he will do just that very soon, then, Hensley, I hope you will make it easy for both of you by letting Peter know you didn't take it all too seriously anyway." She concluded with a brittle little laugh.

Hensley remained with her back toward Margo, fighting back tears in her determination to hide her feelings. She must never allow Margo the satisfaction of knowing what a devastating blow she had given her. There was no way she could deny it—some of it did after all contain a note of truth. She thought of the countless times Peter had said: "This is what Allan wants for you." Why, even the other night by the Christmas tree, he had said how happy Allan would be knowing the two of them were together. Oh, dear God! she thought.

She felt the cool touch of Margo's hand on her arm. "You will think about what I've said, won't you?" She took her hand away. "Well, I must join my friends and take in the party. I haven't even said hello to the host yet." With these banal words, she was gone.

Hensley blessed the sudden quiet of the small room, coveting solitude to face her anguished thoughts. It could be true! All of Peter's thoughtfulness and caring could be fostered by his wish to carry out Allan's plans for her well-being rather than by his own emotional involvement. Allan had wanted not only financial security for her, but also had hoped to provide a place for her to identify with and belong—and a loving relationship to enfold her. Did Peter feel an obligation to provide all of this, and was he only trying to convince himself that it was what he wanted as well? She touched the copper nugget at the hollow of her throat. It pulsed against her fingers. One thought stabbed her with pain. Peter had never told her he loved her!

She walked slowly out of the library. At the foot of the staircase she paused. From the living room she heard Craig's guitar as he started the refrain of "Heart-song": "My heart knows just regret—of a love I can't forget—A love that faded and went wrong—"

She stumbled against the stair and fell to one knee, tears blinding her eyes. She pulled herself up and climbed step by step, feeling her way by sliding her hand along the smooth surface of the stair rail. "The joy of love's refrain—is over and the pain is all that lingers on." The poignant words of the love song echoed sadly in her ears.

"Emma, have you seen my girl?" Peter pushed through the swinging door into the kitchen with his usual rugged force, causing the door to fan the air. Emma looked up from the tray of sliced turkey she was refilling for the buffet table.

"Depends on which one of your girls you mean."

"Very amusing, Emma dear," he countered glibly.

"Well, you do manage to keep yourself so aloof and free of permanent ties. I actually was not aware that you had *a girl!*" She reached for sprigs of parsley to garnish the meat tray.

"There you go again, hinting that I should find a nice girl and settle down." He began to nibble on some scraps of white meat, pulling them from the area under the wing bones.

"Yes, Peter, I have mentioned something to that effect from time to time," she baited him, with a mischievous gleam in her eyes. "It's an old lady's prerogative."

"Well, old lady"—he grinned at her—"I am now informing you that I have found the right girl!"

"That's nice," Emma teased him with her casual response. "Could it be anyone I know?" Fluffing her hair, she smiled up at him.

"You damn well know it's Hensley, of course. The hell of it is, you probably knew it before I did." His wide grin lit up his entire face. "That's what I get for having an all-seeing, all-knowing secretary." He shook his head at her. "And that's only the half of it." He laughed. "You probably will now take full credit for having arranged the whole thing."

Emma's gray-blue eyes twinkled with barely suppressed laughter. "Well, Peter, didn't I?"

He leaned down and kissed her on the forehead. "I salute you, Emma Carlson. You've done it again. Not only are you completely indispensable to Merrick Copper, but to me too. Furthermore, you never let me forget it. Now, please go find Hensley for me while I get the last of the guests in to that buffet table so we can wind up this party." He gave Emma a gentle shove. Glancing at his watch, he saw it was even later than he thought. He should give Reilly his check and let the fellow get back to the motel.

Peter's gaze took in the living room as he returned. The crowd was beginning to thin out, but there was no sign of Hensley. Where could she be? It wasn't like her not to be close by where she could hear her country-western singer. The thought amused him, and it also thrust some pleasant, exciting notions into his mind. After all, it had been those songs of Reilly's that had brought Hensley clashing against him. He smiled inwardly, remembering how the verbal conflict between them had become so delightfully physical the other afternoon in his office.

Suddenly, as if the area were devoid of people, Peter saw nothing else in the room but the Christmas tree he and Hensley had decorated. The emotion-charged events of that night flooded over him. He had no doubts about the powerful attraction which existed between the two of them. Also, he knew Hensley felt it as strongly as he did. He only needed to give her time and she would accept the rightness of their being together. Perhaps tonight . . . He raked his hand through his hair and gave a sudden jerk at his shirt collar; it hugged his neck, making him perspire. He'd be glad to get the opportunity to take off his tie. He detested the constriction of a dress shirt and tie. The corners of his mouth quirked in a smile, for he knew full well what he really wanted was to have the party over and spend the remainder of Christmas Eve alone with Hensley. He rubbed his hand across his forehead. It was hot in this room—and just where could Hensley be?

"Well, at last! I thought my favorite host would never get around to me." Margo put her hand on Peter's arm. "It's a nice party, Peter, and everyone is having a good time."

"Ummm—good." He focused his attention reluctantly on Margo's bright flow of words.

"Peter, you will join all of us later, won't you? We're going to the Bradley's, and you know you're invited." She kept her hand resting on his arm. "The old crowd is going to Big Sky to ski for three days, leaving the day after Christmas. We'll settle all the final arrangements tonight."

He felt the pressure of her fingers, and her eyes seemed to plead with him to acquiesce. "I'm sorry, Margo, I have a number of things to do here. Please understand," he added. He wanted to make it all easy for her; he owed her that.

"I'd counted on it being like other years," she said softly. "You and me making the party rounds together." She sighed, shrugging her lovely shoulders. "Well, if your plans change and you see your way clear to come, I'll be there." The inflection in her voice seemed to hold out an invitation to him to join her, as if she believed he would be inclined to do so. She has total self-assurance, he thought, and at this point in their relationship he found this somehow disquieting.

"At any rate, you'll come skiing with us, like always? It wouldn't be the same without you, Peter." Margo gave him no chance to respond, but letting her manicured nails trail along his arm lightly, she added, "I left a package for you on your desk, something to wear next week at Big Sky. Merry Christmas!" She looked at him for another moment, then turned to rejoin her friends.

Rubbing his hand across his upper lip, he made his way to the group near the fireplace and joined their conversation. The party was drawing to an end.

A short time later, as Peter opened the front door to allow the last of the party guests to leave, Georgie Girl came bounding in from out of the cold December night. The dog rubbed up against Peter's legs to express her joy at finally having him to herself.

"Parties aren't for you, are they, Georgie?" he said, scratching behind her ears, a caress the animal responded to with an affectionate lick of her master's hand.

With the party over, Emma was occupied emptying ashtrays and gathering up the remaining glasses.

"Hey, let that go," Peter called to her. "I'll straighten up later. You've already done the lion's share of the work around here all evening." He pushed his hand through his hair in a gesture of weariness. "Join me in the library, Emma. I want to call Hensley's apartment again. For the life of me, I can't figure out why, or for that matter when, she left the party tonight."

The repeated ringing of her unanswered phone made a hollow sound in his ear. Anxious thoughts began eroding his plans of spending Christmas Eve alone with Hensley. He felt as a child must feel watching the tide, bit by bit, dissolve the complex sand castle he has made, knowing that another time he might not be able to make one quite so tall, so royal.

Emma came in from the kitchen with two steaming mugs of coffee. "That smells great, and I sure need it. I want to unwind and figure out where Hensley went and bring her back!" He took a swallow of coffee, welcoming the feel of the hot liquid as it eased the tenseness in his throat. "Emma, it sure isn't like her to leave without a word to you or me."

"I agree, Peter, but yet, with the party in full swing, she may not have had an opportunity," Emma said, sinking down in one of the two leather chairs and pushing first one black pump and then the other off, letting them drop beside the chair. "Ummm, much better," she sighed, wiggling her toes. "Say, I bet she drove Craig Reilly back into town. He doesn't have a car, you know."

"No, she didn't do that. I missed her much earlier. I'm sure she was gone before I gave Craig his check." He drank his coffee, regarding Emma thoughtfully. "Besides, I think I remember he mentioned something about having borrowed a car from someone at the motel." Peter furrowed his forehead in a frown.

"I've seen an angry bull who looked more relaxed than you do," Emma said, shaking her head at him. "I'm sure there's a simple explanation. She'll call or come back anytime now."

"God, I hope so! I don't like the idea of my girl running out on me. I don't like it one bit!" He growled, scratching his chin.

"Maybe"—Emma's voice was thoughtful—"maybe that's exactly what she did do—run out on you. She is afraid of involvement. You remember she ran away from that boss of hers in Ironville. Isn't it possible, Peter, if she felt she was getting too involved with you, rather than commit herself, she decided to run away again?" Emma shook her head as if the thought saddened her.

"I don't buy it—I can't buy it at all!" His voice was adamant. "I'm not a kid, you know? I'm thirty-two years old and I know a few things about women." Emma's expression caused him to pause. "Stop laughing at me, Emma, you know what I mean!" He let a smile soften the tense lines around his mouth. "Hensley is not afraid of involvement, not with me. I'm certain of that! In some ways we may already be committed to each other. Why else did I wait ten years for her to come out from behind a pair of dark glasses?" He shook his head slowly. "Maybe I didn't know it at the time, but it's true all the same. I waited for her to grow up—to grow up and discover she wanted to be here where we both belong—with copper under our feet and mountains over our heads."

Emma's gray eyes studied him. "It's in the Merrick tradition," she said gently. Her mouth curved in a knowing smile, but her eyes now appeared to look beyond him, as if she were recalling another time. "You sound like your father, Peter. You're very like him, you know." She hesitated, and then, patting the side of her head, she said, "I'm going home now. You get busy tracking down your pretty Hensley." Putting her shoes on, she stood up and smoothed her skirt. "It was a good party and everybody enjoyed it. Another successful Merrick tradition," she added in a tone of pleasure.

"You deserve the majority of the credit there," Peter said, walking with her to the door, his arm affectionately around her shoulders. "You know, when it comes to Merrick traditions, you, dear lady, are the best of all of them." He leaned over and kissed her cheek. "Merry Christmas, Emma."

"Merry Christmas to you, young Peter," she answered, her voice so soft it was almost a whisper.

Closing the door after her, he was thinking it had been years since anyone had called him "young Peter." Growing up, of course, it had been used to distinguish him from his father. He'd been glad of it, as he would have hated going through those years as "junior." Peter Evan Merrick, the father, and young Peter Evan Merrick, the son. It was another of the Merrick traditions. Although it had never been put into words between them, Peter understood the deep affection Emma held for his father—and for "young Peter."

He pulled off his tie, unbuttoning his shirt collar. He glanced at his watch—eight-thirty-five. It was almost an hour since the party ended. The persistent feeling that something might be wrong surfaced more strongly. Deliberately he attempted to push aside his negativism. He needed to take a sensible approach to the problem, make a few phone calls. If she still was not at her apartment, he would call Craig Reilly at the motel, possibly even Ray Holden.

He walked aimlessly through the hall. What if Hensley had started on a foolish whim or errand? It could have taken longer than she anticipated. Impulsive as she often was it was even in the realm of possibility that she had run out for a last-minute Christmas present. Ridiculous as this thought was, he had to smile. Damned if she wouldn't do just such a screwball stunt! Well, whatever, she'd surely call or better yet be back here at the ranch by nine o'clock.

He took the stairs two at a time. Tossing his coat and tie on his bed, he took a tan cashmere sweater from his closet, yanking it over his head. He relished the comfort of being free of his tie. His spirits were definitely improving.

Returning to the living room, he turned off all the lights except for the Christmas tree. He poked at the fire in the fireplace. Wisps of blue-tipped flames danced along the surface of the huge log and orange-red embers cradled the rugged bark where it nested in the grate. Impatience stirred within him. He wanted Hensley to be here with him. Here where he would see her, talk to her, touch her. Restlessly he strode across to the window, peering out beyond the drive to the road. All was dark. There was no flash of headlights to signal an approaching car. Turning away, he decided to try to call her one more time.

In the library he sat down at the desk and pulled the phone toward him. As he did so, he knocked a large Christmas package to one side, thus uncovering a smaller one beneath it. He looked at the two boxes with their brightly wrapped exteriors. Oddly, he felt both drawn and at the same time repelled by the sight of the two dissimilarly shaped packages resting innocently on top of his desk.

Picking up the larger package, he stripped away the wrapping, removed the lid from the box and lifted out a heavy-knit woolen ski sweater. A frown knitted his brows. What had Margo said about leaving a Christmas present for him? Something for him to wear next week at Big Sky, wasn't that it? He pushed the sweater aside. He had no intention of going skiing, not without Hensley. And she had told him she was going to Ironville next week to sell the stamps. Also she had said she had never skied. He scratched his head and smiled to himself. He would teach her to ski—among other things. He pushed himself back from the desk. His grin widened with the varied scope of his thoughts. He felt restless; what he needed was a Scotch. Why didn't the phone ring? The silence around him made him edgy.

"Hey, Georgie Girl," Peter called in a loud voice. As if she had only been waiting to be summoned, the dog appeared in the doorway, her ears alert to receive his commands and her cropped tail wagging like a metronome.

He swung his body around, suddenly curious about the other gift. When he pulled at the green bow, he discovered a card tucked beneath it. It was one of those small, folded gift cards without an envelope. He opened it to see Hensley's round lettered script: "For as long as the mountains stand—I will love you."

His eyes hugged the words, and he read them a

second time. Realization crept along the fringes of his mind. While she had written the words, he had never spoken them to her. Suddenly he was startlingly aware that he had never said "I love you" to Hensley.

For that matter, just what had he ever said—what caring words? He had told her that she belonged here in these mountains, but wasn't that really all? He shook his head as if to jar his memory. Hadn't he said something about her brother wanting her to be here? Even that Allan had brought the two of them together—he recalled saying something to that effect. Had it all been what Allan wanted for her—planned for her? Damn, he thought. Why hadn't he told her of his own feelings? The plans he wanted to make for her—for both of them.

It was Christmas Eve; in just a few more hours it would be Christmas. He would say the words—tell her he loved her. He drew a long breath, struck with the indisputable knowledge that no matter how many times tonight, nor how loudly he might say the words—*I love you*—they would only reverberate against the mountains and echo back in his own ears. It was now painfully clear to him Hensley would not be here to hear them.

Chapter 15

As the plane took off from the Butte airport heading for Great Falls, Hensley was forced, for the first time since she had fled from the party, to consider the full import of what she was doing. When she had recklessly sped away from Peter's house it had seemed the only means of self-preservation. Was it true? Was she an unwanted burden thrust on Peter by a dying friend, as Margo had said? Was Peter making this noble gesture toward her as an end result of his Damon-and-Pythias friendship with her brother? Shuddering sobs shook her body. She buried her face in her hands; closing her eyes, she fought against the tears that filled her throat. Damn! Damn! Damn! she thought, biting her teeth together. Why couldn't Peter fall in love with her? She loved him so much! She touched the pendant around her neck, pressing the disk into the tender hollow of her throat until it bruised her skin. Why did loving Peter hurt so desperately? She reclined her seat and tried to make her mind go blank. She was relieved that she had the seat to herself, for she was too upset to make conversation with a stranger. It was not surprising that the plane had only a handful of passengers. People don't travel on Christmas Eve if they can avoid it. She let her mind linger on these thoughts: it seemed less painful than thinking of Peter.

Arriving in Great Falls, she had only a forty-minute wait for the flight to Duluth. Hurrying through the terminal, she located the nearest phone. She knew she had to let someone know where she had gone. Pushing coins into the change slots, she waited for the operator to get a call through to Emma. It would be far easier to talk to her, for she could not bear the upheaval of hearing Peter's voice.

"Emma . . . it's Hensley. I have only a couple of minutes, and—"

"Hensley, you've had us so worried," Emma interrupted. "Where on earth are you?"

"I'm in Great Falls and I'm due to board my flight to Duluth in just a few minutes. I'm going on to Ironville to take care of things." She raced on, hoping to avoid the questions she knew would be forthcoming from Emma. "I'm sorry if I worried you. I actually decided on the spur of the moment to go on to Minnesota earlier than I had planned, that's all."

"I can't understand what got into you. What possessed you to leave in the very middle of Peter's party, and without a word to either of us?" Emma's usually calm voice was filled with agitation. "Do you know how alarmed we were?"

"I'm sorry, but there's no time to explain. Believe me, I needed to take care of this business in Minnesota. I'll be in touch."

"But it's Christmas! Surely you could have waited. Are you running away?" She raised her voice in reprimand. It struck Hensley that Emma sounded like a scolding mother, and she was touched by the concern in her voice. "Do you want to lose Peter?" Emma asked doggedly.

"I can't lose something I never had in the first place," she replied, swallowing against the catch that came unbidden into her voice.

"Oh, don't be foolish! Peter cares for you very much. I wouldn't be surprised if he did want to marry you."

"He wants to honor the wishes of his dead friend— that's all Peter is trying to do, Emma. Someone pointed this out quite clearly to me tonight!" She hesitated, feeling all her control slipping away. "They're calling my flight; I've got to go," she lied. "Don't worry, I don't need to lean on Peter or anyone else." She forced a confident note into her voice. "Merry . . . Merry Christmas to you . . . and tell Peter Merry Christmas for . . . for me too." She hung up the phone quickly.

It was after midnight when she finally reached Duluth. The next shuttle plane to Ironville was a midmorning flight on Christmas Day. It was just as well. Hensley felt incapable of making the effort to go further tonight. She joined another passenger from the plane and boarded the bus from the motel chain located near the airport.

After checking into a room at the motel, she took a hot shower and swallowed two aspirin. Desolate and weary, she climbed into bed. She closed her eyes, but the back of her eyelids became like a movie screen across which flashed a rerun of the disturbing scenes she had experienced. She opened her eyes quickly. She could not bear to review Margo's actions and words again.

She switched on the light by the bed and gazed around the sleek, impersonal motel room. Her mouth twisted in an ironic smile. She had wanted to stop leaning on others, hadn't she? Well, it was Christmas and she was alone in Minnesota. There was no one to lean on here even if she wanted to. Turning off the light, she buried her face in the pillow, releasing all the tears she had held inside since she had run away from Peter's house.

Chapter 16

Hensley did not try to contact David until late Christmas afternoon. She did not want him to have to rearrange his holiday plans because of her earlier arrival in Ironville. The fact that she had arrived ahead of schedule either aroused no questions in his mind or else he was discreet enough to refrain from comment. Whatever the reason, Hensley was grateful not to have to offer explanations.

"I'll come to the *Journal* office after I get the stamps from the bank in the morning," she told David on the phone.

"Great, and I'll take you out for lunch. We'll

combine business with pleasure; I'm anxious to see you," he said with an affectionate laugh. "Hensley I'm really excited about getting my hands on that pair of Cartier stamps at last!" His voice boomed in her ear.

"I'm pleased too, you know that. Now I'll let you go so you won't be late for your dinner. Merry Christmas—see you tomorrow."

David had told her that he was invited to Christmas dinner with friends. He'd been distressed at the idea of her spending the evening alone. His concern touched her. David made no secret of his feelings for her. How simple it could be now, she thought, if only she cared for David as she did Peter. She squared her shoulders in a determined gesture. It was Christmas and she was alone and that was that. Having cried all her tears last night, she would allow herself no more self-pity. Of course, she was more alone than she had ever been, for Allan was dead and she would never be more to Peter than the sister of his friend. But she could make it on her own—no more leaning and no more tears! She smiled wanly, finding little comfort in the thought.

Immediately after breakfast the following day, she went to the bank to collect the contents of the safe-deposit box.

They were gone! The Canadian stamps were gone! There was not a trace of them. Hensley's hands trembled as she searched the box for the third time. The stamps simply were not there. Tremors of disbelief shivered through her. She kept shaking her head, as if this action could somehow help her make some sense of her frightening discovery.

How could these valuable stamps have been removed? Only Allan's signature or hers would permit entry. She gazed around the tiny cubicle, this confining stall of a room in which she could privately examine her brother's safe-deposit box. The place was suddenly airless. She had to get out of here. She felt as if she were suffocating.

Placing the contents of the box in a zippered portfolio she had brought for this purpose, she hurried out, leaving the green metal container behind. Indeed, she literally ran in her eagerness to escape the cell-like enclosure.

The buzzer sounded its metallic tone as she signaled the vault attendant to open the grilled gate so she could leave. As she approached the desk in the outside area, she fought to control her nerves and focus her mind, to think rationally. Asking to examine the signatures on the entry card, she took time to study it carefully. Other than her own signature this morning, there were only two others dated after May 1 of this year. Allan's lawyer and an official of the bank had inventoried the box after Allan's death. This entry, with authorization, was dated the thirtieth of July. Hensley recalled being informed of this. It had been one of a number of details she had been told concerning the settling of Allan's affairs. The only other earlier signature was Allan's and the date was July 3.

Staring at her brother's handwriting, she tried to remember back to early July. When was it Allan had gone into the hospital that final time? It was after the fourth, she knew—probably it had been about the middle of the month. Yes, she was almost certain it had been about the fourteenth or fifteenth of the month. She bobbed her head involuntarily. She remembered something—Allan had gone out of town over the Fourth of July holiday. He had gone to Duluth; she recalled it quite clearly now. He had been gone perhaps a week and when he returned he hadn't seemed at all well. It was only a few days later that he went into the hospital for blood transfusions—and he had remained in the hospital until his death.

"I'm really confused, and there's something quite

wrong here," she said to the attendant. "I'm very upset, because something is missing from the deposit box." Her voice rose in agitation.

"Perhaps I can help you. Is there some question about the entry card?" the slender woman inquired courteously.

Hensley tapped her finger over the July signature of Allan's. "I see by this that my brother entered the box July third. I don't understand, because he gave me the key to the box before the end of June. It's been in my possession ever since." She held out her hand with the key to confirm her words.

"There are two keys for each box, Miss Travis," she said reassuringly. "Just a minute and I'll check this for you. I need to have you sign a card anyway for you to receive your key refund." Opening a file cabinet, she pulled a card and placed it in front of her on the desk. "I note here"—she nodded—"the second key was turned in by Mr. Travis' lawyer, Steward Parker, on July thirtieth, following the inventory of the box. One of our bank officers, a Mr. Walters, was present at the time. This, of course, is a legal requirement." She smiled politely. "Does this answer your questions?"

"I guess so." Hensley sighed. "At least I understand about the two keys. Thank you very much," she said, turning to go.

"One minute, Miss Travis." Standing up behind her desk, the attendant extended the receipt slip toward Hensley. "Take this to one of the teller windows and you'll receive your key refund."

Taking the piece of paper she offered, Hensley walked away.

She wiped nervous perspiration from her upper lip with a tissue. Undercurrents of anxiety tugged at her mind like a riptide. What was the explanation? Fifty thousand dollars' worth of Canadian stamps certainly did not evaporate into thin air. They were removed from the deposit box somehow and by someone, but how and when and by whom? If she was to get the money for Craig, she must first get some answers.

Pushing through the revolving doors at the bank, she walked rapidly along Main Street to the law offices of Parker and Pratt. She bowed her head against the bitter cold wind that stung her face. Her hands hurt in the freezing air. She thrust one hand in the pocket of her coat, but the other, in which she clutched the black zipper case, remained unprotected. How stupid she had been not to wear gloves, she thought.

The day after Christmas was not one in which a small-town lawyer has a full schedule of appointments, it appeared. This was fortunate for Hensley, for she was becoming more and more upset over the disappearance of the stamps. After a very brief wait she was shown into the book-lined office of the senior partner in the law firm of Parker and Pratt.

"Hensley, my dear, you're a pretty sight for my old eyes," Stewart Parker greeted her warmly. "I had no idea you were in Ironville for Christmas."

"Oh, Mr. Parker, my dad's stamp collection is missing." She blurted the words out at the sight of the stout white-haired gentleman. "Dad's Canadian stamps are gone from the safe-deposit box, and I don't understand how such a thing could happen. You've just got to be able to help me!" Stewart Parker was not only the family legal adviser; he had been a contemporary and close friend of her father's, so Hensley felt no compunction in approaching him with her problems, for she felt he was the only one who might be able to shed some light on the mystery.

"Now, Hensley, calm down for a minute. Take a seat there by my desk and we'll look into this matter." He patted her hand and helped her to a chair. "You're referring to your brother's deposit box, of course?"

"I've just come from the bank; I have everything

from the box here." She indicated the zipper case she now held on her lap. "A valuable collection of stamps that Allan kept there were not in the box." She fingered the portfolio nervously. "I have to locate those stamps, Mr. Parker. Can you help me?"

"I'll certainly try, my dear." He went over to a row of file cabinets across one wall of the room, returning to his desk with a large manila folder. "Now, let me see what I have here in Allan's papers." He took a few minutes to thumb through the folder before handing several sheets to Hensley. "This is the copy of the box inventory I made after Allan died. I'm sure you recall having seen it last summer. Fact is, you initialed it for our records," he added, indicating dates and markings on the pages to her.

"I guess I do remember something like that, but I'm afraid I didn't pay very close attention. It was a difficult time for me, and at best I'm remiss concerning business details." She frowned. "I'm sure I didn't read it carefully." She stopped talking and studied the papers he had given her.

While she read, Stewart Parker took a cigar from a box on his desk. Cutting the end with his penknife, he put it in his mouth without lighting it. He then turned his attention to the remaining contents of the folder.

Hensley looked up. "I see the stamps do not appear on the inventory," she said. "That means they were removed before my brother died." She made it a statement rather than a question. "I wanted to make that clear in my mind."

Stewart Parker nodded. "There is no mention of a stamp collection among Allan's assets. They were not a part of his estate, Hensley."

"Are you saying Allan disposed of those stamps? Sold them or something before he died?" She eyed him closely, impatient for the answers that would end the fears and misgiving building in her mind.

"I can't say. I haven't any knowledge concerning this," he answered. "Your brother arranged for everything to go into a trust for you. This, of course, you know. Our firm did handle the trust, and Allan's friend Merrick was named trustee."

"Do you mean it's possible Allan sold the stamps and placed the money from the sale in trust for me?" She felt she was belaboring the point, but the financial and legal aspects of this confused her.

"Only if he then reinvested the money in stocks or bonds. The assets of the trust are all in various common stocks and a few municipal bonds. No stocks or bonds were added after the trust was set up at the end of April. Unless the stamps were sold before the trust was established, then money resulting from such a sale never became any part of the trust assets." He continued to explain patiently to Hensley, showing her a copy of the trust and pointing out the list of stocks and bonds on the legal document.

"I understand," she said, turning on through the several pages of the trust form. "Peter—I mean, Mr. Merrick—informed me that the money I receive each month as an allowance is from investment income." She allowed a wry smile to accompany her words. "He made this entirely clear to me, quite recently in fact. He explained this was the reason why I can't obtain a large sum without something being sold from the trust." Leaning forward, she returned the trust papers to the lawyer. "This is the reason I'm so anxious about the stamps." She raised her voice slightly. "I plan to sell one particular pair to raise money for a personal reason."

Steward Parker's bright eyes held an amused glint. "Sounds like this Westerner, Merrick, knows how to keep a wise rein on more than one kind of filly!" He chuckled at his little joke. "You should be grateful for the trustee's caution, Hensley. It is important for your

167

future that the assets of the trust be kept intact. In these inflated times your trust income would support your basic needs, but not permit you to indulge in extravagances."

"I know." She shrugged. "Peter talks in the same vein you do." She sighed, thinking she actually had learned nothing that would explain the disappearance of the stamp collection. She thought of the night in June when Allan had warned her to safeguard her legacy.

"Keep the collection intact," he had said. "Sell it only if you need it for an emergency." She chewed the corner of her lip thoughtfully. Allan had said something else. "The Canadian series will be yours, however, and you may use it any way you like. Sell any or all of it, if it should be really important to you." She could almost hear him saying this. Suddenly she remembered he had also said, "I would do the same—for a great enough cause."

Allan had given her the key to the deposit box that night in June. The stamps had been in the bank then, but now they were gone. Brushing the palms of her hands together in a gesture of finality, she rose from her chair. "I mustn't take any more of your time, Mr. Parker. Thank you for trying to help, and let me wish you a happy New Year."

"The very same to you, my dear," he said, helping her with her coat. "Are you back in Ironville to stay, I hope?"

"Only for a few days. I have a job in Anaconda. I should return before New Year's." Mentioning Anaconda disturbed her further; her inner thoughts wiped the thin smile from her face. She buttoned and belted her coat with perfunctory haste.

"Brrrrr!" She hugged herself against the biting wind as she left the building. Turning up her coat collar to shield her neck, she walked with brisk steps in the direction of the newspaper office. It did appear that the legacy of stamps had vanished—poof—like a soap bubble in the air. Logically, they had to have been removed from the safe-deposit box by Allan, using his key and signing his name for entry. Logic and reason seemed of small importance at this moment. The immediate effect of no stamps—no money—was that she could not give Craig the financial aid she had promised him. She would have to telephone him and tell him what had happened. She dreaded the thought of disappointing him. Would he have to postpone going to Nashville? Would it destroy his big chance?

Regrets crowded her thoughts. Helping Craig had been the one happy hope that had sustained her since she left Anaconda. Was even that to be denied her now?

She was freezing cold. Her eyes stung with icy tears. How could Allan have taken the stamps without telling her? He must have faced an emergency—something vital and urgent. But if that had been the case, wouldn't he have explained it to her? What possible need would be so great as to require his taking the entire collection? Part of them, yes; after all, half would be rightfully his. But all $50,000 worth?

She quickened her steps until she was almost running. That early-summer night when Allan gave her the key, the stamps had been safely stored in the deposit box. What could have happened later? He entered the box on July 3; she'd seen his signature on the card this morning. Did he take the stamps out then? Allan felt so strongly about preserving the collection, he couldn't have disposed of them casually. What reason could he have had? Would she ever find out? She began to run as fast as she could. She was not at all sure she wanted to discover the answers.

Chapter 17

The rapid staccato sounds of a typewriter greeted her as
she entered the newspaper office. Hensley stood in the
doorway, not removing her coat. Every inch of her
body felt cold. She knew it was more than the freezing
walk from Mr. Parker's. Everything she had discovered
this morning left her chilled with doubts and threatened
to mar her memories of her brother.

"Hensley, you look frozen! Come in my office and
take a chair near the warm-air vent. I'll get you some
hot coffee," David said, taking her hands and rubbing
them between his to warm them.

"Oh, David, what a bleak and hopeless mess," she
said as she poured out the events of the morning to him
in anguished words.

He listened, questioning her carefully about details.
His initial expression of incredulity changed to one of
speculation.

"Hensley, we're going to get to the bottom of this!
I'll swear it smacks to me of some kind of rip-off," he
said, taking a final drag on a cigarette and then putting
it out in the ashtray.

"The whole thing is so unlike my brother. I can't
understand it." She shook her head sadly.

"I'm thinking that there was strong pressure brought
to bear on him from some quarter. I'm going to nose
around; maybe I can inveigle the stamp dealer in
Duluth into disclosing the owner of those Canadian
stamps he was seeking a buyer for."

"Do you think you could? It would help. At least I think I'd feel better if I knew whether it was my dad's collection that was being sold," she said, propping her chin on her hand and gazing thoughtfully at David.

He put on his glasses and pulled the phone across his desk toward him. Obtaining the number he was seeking from directory assistance, he dialed.

"Mr. McIntyre? David Gillette in Ironville. You contacted me a few weeks ago about a Canadian series of stamps. . . . Right, those are the ones. . . . No, I have the Victoria and Albert rose issue; it's the Jacques Cartier pair I'm seeking. Fact is, I'm quite eager to arrange to buy. . . . Um-huh . . . yes." David wagged his head as he listened.

"Well . . . how soon do you expect to have it available? . . . You think not?" he said, jutting his chin out. "What if you gave me the name of the owner and let me contact him direct? . . . Is that right?"

Hensley could see David's eyes spark with interest. He glanced at her and nodded his head. He's evidently making some progress she thought. She could feel excitement building inside her.

"What law firm is that?" she heard David ask. "Dammit, McIntyre, it surely does sound complicated for a legitimate sale!" David pulled off his glasses, displaying his irritation. He tapped them angrily on top of his desk as he continued talking. "I'll tell you what I think," he growled into the phone. "It sure as *hell* has all the earmarks of the Travis collection! . . . You bet your sweet life it does!"

He replaced his glasses slowly and leaned back in his chair. "I agree with you. . . . You certainly should have been informed. Ah, yes . . . yes indeed."

David's voice began to take on a friendly, conspiratorial tone. "You know, young Allan Travis inherited the collection, and it's quite possible he may have made arrangements with the law firm you mentioned for the sale of those stamps." He hesitated. "Devil of it is, Allan Travis died the end of July. . . . Right, here in Ironville."

"Now, I happen to be personally acquainted with his sister, Hensley . . ." He began to speak in his characteristic strident tones. "I'm sure you will agree with me, it is only right she get an opportunity to buy any part of the collection that has not already been sold—outside of the Cartier stamps, of course." He chuckled. "Miss Travis knows I want those particular stamps for my own collection. I've been trying to get my hands on the Cartier set for over ten years now." He laughed again and winked at Hensley.

She shook her head at him. What an act he's putting on, she thought.

David was grinning now. "Yes, as a matter of fact, she happens to be here in Ironville for the holidays. . . . Could you do that? I'd really appreciate it, but she's only here for a few more days, so if you could get right back to me . . . O.K., then, I'll wait to hear from you! . . . You bet. . . . Indeed it has!"

David turned from the phone with a smug look of satisfaction on his features. "Without a doubt that guy knows more than he's willing to divulge to me, but I believe we'll get some answers." He smiled at Hensley. "And in short order, too, so wipe that frown off your pretty face, honey."

Still frowning, Hensley chewed lightly at the corner of her lip. "David, you know I can't buy back any of those stamps. Whatever made you tell the man that?"

"Sure, I know that." He ran his hand through his thick red hair. "I just tossed it at him—sort of bait, you could say. Damn if he didn't jump at it, too!" He chuckled, throwing his head back in that confident manner of his. "I'm convinced McIntyre knows those earlier stamps he sold were a part of the Travis collection. Furthermore, he hinted that the remaining pairs of stamps will either go on the market very soon or else they won't be offered at all."

"What do you mean—not at all?" She leaned forward in her chair, surprised at David's statement.

"Just that, Hensley. The dealer said the first stamps, the Victoria and Albert he first offered me, were turned over to him by the lawyer who represents the owner of the stamps. He claims he doesn't know who the owner is, and I believe him."

"O.K., but what has that got to do with whether the rest will be sold right away or not at all?"

"It seems this lawyer had at first told McIntyre that the stamps would be offered a pair at a time, with intervals of as long as a year or two between offerings. Then, in the past few weeks, the lawyer approached him with the proposition of selling the remainder of the collection to a single buyer, in the hope it would bring a greater sum, premium price so to speak, from an individual. McIntyre assumed from this that unless he could find a buyer interested in the whole package, the stamps would be withdrawn from the present market altogether." David reached for a cigarette, obviously satisfied with the information gleaned from his call.

"Now I understand why you told him I was interested in buying back the collection." She rubbed her forehead. She felt the beginnings of a headache pressing over her eyes. "I'm sorry you lied to him," she said, closing her eyes and hunching her shoulders to relieve the tight feeling in her neck.

The past few hours, her trip to the bank, the meeting with Stewart Parker and now David's call to the stamp dealer—everything she had learned today weighed on her thoughts. These happenings triggered her memory, touching off too many sad recollections. How many times had Allan reiterated his hope that she would keep the stamp collection intact? Now—he had been the one to dispose of her legacy! How could he have arranged all of this with never a word to her? At least he had owed her an explanation before he took what should have been her rightful share of their father's stamps. Whatever Allan's reasons, his needs—why hadn't he trusted her enough to believe she would understand?

Tears pressed at the back of her eyes. With a gesture of frustration, Hensley got up, and leaning against the edge of David's desk, said solemnly, "I wish I'd never heard of these wretched stamps. They're causing nothing but pain and misunderstandings." She straightened, looking away from David's face. "I refuse to let myself harbor ugly thoughts against my brother. The stamps were his—all of them. He had every right to do anything with them he felt it necessary to do. I'm not going to question his motives any further." She looked back at David. "The truth is, I think I'm afraid to learn what might have prompted his actions." She brushed at her eyes with her fingertips, "I might really have cause to cry then, who knows?"

David stopped smoking and walked around his desk to her.

"The irony of it all is," she said, a wry smile twisting her lips, "I only wanted the money from the stamps to indulge a dream I had. I wanted to play Lady Bountiful and provide a measure of support to another person." She shrugged. "I liked the idea of for once having someone lean on me." She gave a ragged laugh and added, "It didn't last long, did it? I'm already back, leaning on you again, David."

He put his arms around her. "You're just letting your emotions play leapfrog with your good sense, Hensley. A man wants his woman to turn to him for help and support, don't you know that?" He tilted her chin, forcing her to look directly into his eyes. "You may not realize it, but you're the kind of woman who would be a real partner in a relationship. You would lean, yes, but also you would support the man you love." He smiled at her. "I for one would like nothing better than to lean on you—anytime and anyplace." He tightened his arms around her. "You know how I feel about you, because I certainly never made any secret about wanting you! Will you stay here in Ironville with me—lean on me permanently?"

Hensley moistened her lips and drew in her breath to speak, but she couldn't make the words come. David's blue eyes concentrated on her face. Whether she made a reflex movement or if he simply eased his embrace, she did not know, but after a few seconds he released her.

"D-David . . ." Her voice trembled. "I want you to please . . . please understand . . ."

He tossed his red head in a gesture of bravado. "I do understand, Hensley," he said in a voice that was quiet, for him. "And that's the hell of it!"

Chapter 18

It was late in the afternoon when Wayne Endicott, a lawyer in Duluth, telephoned Hensley. Their conversation was brief. He told her nothing other than the fact that he had been retained by Allan early in July of this year and that he had the Canadian series of stamps in his possession.

"At your earliest convenience, Miss Travis, I'd like to meet with you here at my office. Would tomorrow afternoon be agreeable?"

"I'll take a morning flight and can be there at one-thirty, or anytime later in the afternoon. I'm anxious to settle all of this, Mr. Endicott." She wondered why she had made this superfluous remark.

His own manner was so businesslike and he spoke in such succinct phrases that she felt she should have followed his pattern.

"One-thirty is fine. I will see you then." Their conversation ended.

On the flight to Duluth, Hensley experienced ambivalent feelings regarding the approaching appointment with Wayne Endicott. There was a kind of relief in realizing that this whole affair of the stamps was about to be explained. On the other hand, she felt almost afraid of acquiring a total knowledge of Allan's actions. One area of her mind seemed to warn her that she might be happier not discovering everything.

After she had talked to the lawyer yesterday, her first thought had been to telephone Peter, to tell him what had happened, to discuss it with him; but she had let too much time go by. Peter had made several attempts to talk to her, calling the newspaper and leaving messages. She had avoided talking with him and refused to return his calls. She had made excuses to herself, saying she was too upset, even too confused to talk to Peter, since the encounter with Margo.

Now she would welcome his advice, his suggestions regarding this meeting with the lawyer. She felt reticent to ask; after all, she would then be leaning on him again, asking him to aid "Allan's little sister" one more time.

She could have asked David to come to Duluth with her, to be her backup man when she met with Mr. Endicott, but she would simply be leaning again. What was she afraid of? This time, for once in her life, couldn't she handle it alone? Couldn't she cope?

The amenities over, Hensley sat down in the chair the lawyer indicated. Crossing her legs, she arranged her skirt over her knees. She experienced a vague sense of surprise upon discovering Wayne Endicott to be a

176

man in his late twenties. From his manner and tone of voice on the phone yesterday, she had envisioned an older, less affable man. In the chrome-and-vinyl surroundings of his contemporary office, he was at once both talkative and genial. He saw that she had a comfortable chair, offered her a cigarette, which she declined, and coffee, which she accepted.

"Cream and sugar?" he asked, placing a tray containing two cups of coffee and packets of sugar and powdered creamer on the round conference table in front of her.

"Uh, no, thank you—just black," she said, taking the cup he handed to her.

"I realize you must be wondering why I had not been in touch with you when it happened, Miss Travis," he said. "The truth is, my secretary did try to reach your apartment in Anaconda the morning after Christmas. Later that day we contacted the Merrick Copper Company and were informed that you were out of the city, in fact in Minnesota." The lawyer smiled as he leaned forward to empty a sugar packet into his cup. "By a fortunate coincidence, James McIntyre, the stamp dealer, contacted me before I had tracked you down in Ironville." He laughed pleasantly. "I must say, his call certainly facilitated my locating you."

Hensley stared at the dark liquid in her cup. For some reason she felt she must have missed some of Wayne Endicott's beginning words. She blinked her eyes, feeling annoyed with herself for her confusion. She was paying close attention; what had she missed? she wondered. Placing her cup on the table, she looked directly at him as he continued talking.

"It is tragic and of course it saddened all of us. She worked for this office, as you probably know. We all thought a great deal of Karen."

"Karen?" She stared at him. "What do you mean—Karen? Karen who?" she blurted out in bewilderment.

"Karen Blake," he said quickly, his forehead lined in a frown. "I'm referring to the death of Karen Blake, Miss Travis." Wayne Endicott stared back at her, shaking his head slowly. "She died Christmas night. I . . . I thought, of course, you knew."

"No—why, no, I didn't. You see, I really did not know her. She was a friend of my brother's." She shook her head. "I'm sorry, however, I . . . I'm sorry to hear this." She put her hand to her throat; her fingers felt ice cold against the warm flesh of her neck. She felt numbed by his words.

The lawyer continued to frown at her, his lips now pressed firmly together, which made his expression at once stern and disapproving. Hensley rubbed her throat, feeling suddenly apprehensive.

"Umm, I see. Then it's only the matter of the stamps that concerns you?" His voice had taken on a noticeable coolness. "Let me assure you, Miss Travis, there is no question of your having to purchase the remaining stamps in the Canadian series! They will now revert to you!"

She winced inwardly. Wayne Endicott's manner toward her had become brusque and decidedly unfriendly. Why, he believes I'm totally unfeeling about Karen Blake's death, she thought. That must be the reason for the change in his attitude. What did he mean—the stamps would revert? Revert from what—from whom?

She felt a little dazed. "Please—I'm sorry, but I don't understand. I really don't."

"I will explain," he said curtly. "Your brother's arrangements allowed me to sell the stamps, one pair at a time. This original plan was for a very definite purpose. He intended to make absolutely certain that money would be available to cover the medical and hospital costs at the birth of the child, and afterward, of course, for the child's care and education."

"*Child?*" Hensley gaped at the attorney in astonishment, "What child? Whose child?"

"You did know, didn't you? Your brother is the father of Karen Blake's baby!"

She couldn't speak. Swaying forward, she gripped the sides of her chair, her arms stiff and her fingers trembling. Unbidden, the vision of emerald-green eyes shining with unshed tears flashed through her mind. That long-ago April afternoon, had Karen come seeking Allan to tell him she was pregnant—pregnant with his child?

"I must apologize, Miss Travis. I've handled this badly. Indeed, I am sorry." He spoke to her in terse phrases. "I naturally presumed you knew all about this and that, in fact, it was your reason for being in Minnesota. I thought you had come for the funeral."

Hensley felt as if she were moving downward, away from the sound of his voice. She must have attempted to stand up; she could not remember making any movement at all. But suddenly Wayne Endicott's hands were on her arms, bracing her weaving body to keep her from falling.

Wayne Endicott now showed her every consideration. He apologized again. "I realize now that you were unaware of the circumstances involving your brother and Karen. I know that all of this coming at once is a shock to you."

She nodded and sank down again in the chair. "I knew nothing—nothing." She shook her head. "Allan talked to me once about Karen," she said, staring into space, "but I only saw her twice. I barely knew her at all."

"She was a very insecure person, and fortunately your brother understood this. Karen lived with anxieties. We who worked here with her were aware of this," Wayne Endicott stated, his tone matter-of-fact. Hensley knew he was not making excuses for Karen, only attempting to explain her innate attitudes.

Hearing his words, she recalled the last night she spent talking with Allan in his hospital room. Hadn't he said much the same thing concerning Karen? He had said she was afraid of cancer—and of dying. Maybe she had been afraid of life as well?

As if he had read Hensley's mind, Wayne Endicott said, "Your brother had reason to fear Karen might seek an abortion—even take her own life."

She felt as if she were finally seeing the last several pieces of a puzzle fit into place. That last July night in the hospital—she knew it had been Karen on the phone with Allan. Had Karen told him she was contemplating an abortion? Was that what had upset Allan so terribly? Had she later called back to tell Allan that she would not harm the expected child or herself? Surely it was such a message that Karen had been so anxious to make certain Allan had received before he died!

"Dear God," she prayed in the silence of her thoughts. "Let Allan have known the truth. He wished so fervently to leave something of himself behind—let him have known!"

She drew in her breath suddenly and looked intently at the lawyer. "The baby—is it a boy or a girl?"

"A boy—Travis Blake—born December twenty-third. He's healthy and fine, Miss Travis," he added with a smile.

"Oh, I want to see him—now—this afternoon. Could I?" she asked eagerly.

Wayne Endicott glanced at his watch. "Of course you can. If I drive you to the hospital right now, you can get there while the visiting hours for the nursery are in effect."

"Won't that be an imposition? I don't want to take you away from your office. I'll take a cab," she added quickly.

"Nonsense! I have an errand to run anyway, and I can easily drop you at the hospital on the way. I have a few more details to talk over with you, and we can discuss them in the car."

Wayne Endicott's voice was quietly compassionate as he explained the legal aspects concerning Allan's son. "Karen Blake had no family, no brothers or sisters that is, and her parents are dead. You realize, however, that if you don't feel you can accept the responsibility of a newborn child, Miss Travis, this is certainly understandable. You do have the legal choice of placing the child for adoption. It is important for you to consider this possibility," he added gently.

Not take Allan's son—not keep him, care for him? It was unthinkable. "There is nothing to consider, Mr. Endicott. He is my family. Why, this child has no one but me. He and I are all that remains—the only two people remaining of the Travis bloodline," she stated firmly.

The lawyer looked at her, his eyes narrowed in serious thought. "The boy could complicate your life to a great extent, you know that? You're not married—the responsibility you're undertaking . . . well . . . give it some consideration. There is no rush to decide. Take all the time you need." He paused; then, in a slightly less solemn tone he said, "The baby is only five days old, there is no reason he cannot remain in the hospital another day or two before either you take him or he is placed in a foster home to await adoption."

"I appreciate what you're trying to say, I really do," she said quietly. "Believe me, I know what it is to be alone. When my brother died last summer, I was left without any family. Travis Blake is Allan's son. He has some family. He has me." She smiled. "He needs me, Mr. Endicott, and I want to arrange to take him back to Anaconda with me as soon as possible."

They were approaching the hospital entrance. "I'll come to your hotel with some papers for you to sign, and I'll bring the Canadian stamps after six o'clock this evening," he said with a firm handshake as Hensley got out of his car. "Looks like that will about wind up our business." He grinned. "You came after stamps and you're winding up with a bit more."

She laughed nervously, an excited mixture of emotions coursing through her. "And my nephew is of greater importance than the stamps!" Closing the car door, she turned and ran quickly up the sidewalk and into the hospital.

For a moment, on entering, she felt the remembered sensations of dread and sadness. There were the same almost repulsive antiseptic odors and the sterile silence she recalled from those July days in the Ironville hospital. Pushing these unpleasant impressions from her thoughts, she entered the elevator. This was a happy visit. She had come to greet a small new life, not to say farewell to an ending one.

On the maternity floor, there was a vital air of expectancy. The corridor was bright; cheerful smiles seemed as much a part of the nurses' uniforms as their starched white caps. Visitors carrying bouquets of flowers or packages wrapped in pink or blue paper lent the atmosphere of a party in pastels.

Hensley peered through the observation window as the nurse lifted the baby from his basket and held him up so she could take her first look at Travis Blake. She smiled, seeing his tiny clenched fists waving in the air like a tough young pugilist. If only Allan could be standing here too, looking with joy and pride at his son. Hensley blinked at the mist that for a moment blurred her sight. At least Karen had held on to life long enough to give their child the name she had chosen for him.

It was after five when Hensley got back to her hotel room. She called the airline and made a flight reservation for two days later. She added two more items to the list she had been keeping of things she must buy tomorrow in preparation for Travis. She had to admit to herself, she was more than a little nervous at the thought of her first trip on an airplane with a week-old baby.

She had promised David that she would call him after seeing the lawyer. She had to let him know her plans. She sighed. She knew David so well; when he learned about Allan's son, she knew he would want to take over and try to talk her into staying in Ironville. She shook her head. David would do his utmost to convince her that she couldn't cope with a baby without his support. Reluctant to talk to him now, she decided to wait and call him after Mr. Endicott brought the stamps. Hopefully David would be so excited about getting the Cartier stamp at last that he wouldn't press her to change her mind about returning to Montana.

She made a little clicking sound of pleasure. Thank goodness she had not called Criag yesterday when she had been certain she would never see the stamps. Everything was working out. David would have the pair of stamps and Craig would have the money she had promised him. She felt a moment of elation, but it faded almost as quickly as it came. She knew her problems concerning Peter were compounded by all that had happened today.

She pushed her hair back from her cheek and deliberately moved away from the phone. Even if she did want to call and talk to Peter—tell him about Allan's son—probably he had gone to Big Sky skiing with Margo and his other friends. Tears of anguish clawed at her throat and brimmed over from her eyes. Stomping across the room, she flung herself down on the bed, angered by her own emotional contrariness.

There was a rapid knocking on her door. It must be Wayne Endicott, she thought. She got up from the bed, pulling at her skirt to straighten it, as the two sharp knocks sounded again.

Releasing the lock, she opened the door. Peter's rugged frame filled the doorway. She stared at him in shocked surprise. "How did you find—what are you doing here? Why did you come?" She gripped the doorknob to steady herself. She could actually feel the blood drain from her face.

"Why not?" he said. "And is that any way to welcome a guy who has tracked you down all over the state of Minnesota?" Peter's dark eyes were frowning, but he obviously was trying to keep his voice even and controlled. He reached out to take hold of her hand as he added, "Where else should I be but with you, Hensley?"

She stepped back and to the side of the door to let him enter. She needed to maintain some distance between them while she struggled to get some control of herself. "I . . . I thought you and Margo had gone skiing together at Big Sky."

"I imagined she had made you think something of the sort." He narrowed his eyes, giving his face a glowering scowl. "Isn't it time you stopped giving credence to anything Margo says? Forget her, Hensley. I certainly have."

A dozen different emotions erupted inside her. She could not begin to sort and separate one from another in an instant. But given time she could, and until then it was enough that Peter's words had erased Margo's image as decisively as a fresh new eraser wipes a chalk line from a blackboard.

Before she could say a word, Peter continued, "Now, in answer to your question as to why I came, I'll tell you. After several attempts to reach you by phone in Ironville, I decided that if I wanted to talk to you, I'd have to fly out and lasso you myself." He smiled at her and reached for her hand again.

"But how did you know I was in Duluth?" She pushed the door firmly shut with her free hand, and with her other one still pressed tightly into his, steered him to the only chair in the room. Pulling gently free of his grasp, she sat down opposite him on the edge of the bed. "How did you ever find me?" How thin and tense her voice sounded. She found it difficult to form words much less sentences, for her heart felt as if it were lodged in her throat.

"Fortunately, I called David from the airport when I arrived in Duluth this afternoon. He, of course, told me you had left Ironville and were meeting with this lawyer, Wayne Endicott. The rest was easy." He inclined his head toward her, smiling that warm, disarming smile of his. "I called Endicott's office and had quite a talk with him. He told me you were staying at this hotel. After that I got a cab and got here as fast as I could."

"Oh . . . Peter," she stammered. "Did he tell you . . . ? Do you know all that has happened?" Her voice caught on small choking sounds of emotion. She glanced away from him, fingering the copper chain around her neck.

Peter nodded. "Endicott filled me in. It's sad about Karen Blake," he said quietly. "I was sorry to hear about it, but not really surprised somehow. That girl had so many fears, I doubt she possessed the will to live."

"Surely you were surprised about Allan having a son?" Her eyes were wide and questioning.

"That fact did surprise me." He leaned toward her and took both of her hands in his. Chuckling, he added, "The ol' miner came through a winner. By God, he certainly left something of himself behind after all." Peter's dark eyes crinkled with laughter. "Dammit, Hensley, your brother has gotten ahead of me again."

"How's that?" She was so conscious of the warmth of

Peter's hands, she hadn't listened closely to what he had been saying.

Peter wagged his head, still laughing. "Allan has a son to show for his thirty-two years, and all I've got is a lonely ranch in the Montana mountains and a hunk of copper." Letting go of her hands, he jumped up and sat down very close beside her on the bed. "I don't have anyone who'll lean on me." He had ceased laughing, and his voice was suddenly low-pitched and serious.

He was disturbingly near, and she felt an absurd desire to rest her head against his shoulder. "You'll have to do something about that, won't you?" she asked quickly, looking down at her hands, now clenched tightly in her lap.

"I intend to," he said, lifting her chin and turning her face up to his. "In fact, I intend to do two things about it."

"Wh-what two things?" she stammered, her face flushing beneath Peter's scrutiny.

"I want to take Allan's son to the ranch where he belongs. Where he can grow up surrounded by the mountains as Allan would have wanted."

Hensley caught her breath in a surge of emotion, looking at Peter, her eyes luminous with tears.

"But before I can do that," he added, "I intend to tell the girl I love just how deeply and completely I *do* love her." He cupped her face tenderly in his strong hands. "Then I shall take her in my arms and show her how I want her, how I need her to fill my life because she is more important to me than anyone or anything. Perhaps, if I am able to convince her that my love is forever like the mountains—maybe then, she will stop running away from me." His eyes darkened with desire, and tipping her face up, he put his lips to hers. His kiss was filled with the wealth of love and the deep longing he felt for her.

Joyously she kissed him back with a yearning that seemed to rise from an overfull heart to fill her entire being. For now there was such elation spreading over her, she was wrapped in a wondrous feeling of fulfillment. Moving eagerly into his arms, she reached up, locking her hands securely around his neck. Catching her breath in a sigh, she whispered softly against his lips, "Who's running, Peter?"

If you have enjoyed *Where Mountains Wait,* why not read an exciting Silhouette Romance set in France

SHADOW AND SUN: Mary Carroll

Britt Ryan had never dreamed that her flair for photography would take her to France to visit the historic Chateau de Laon. Now she had only to pin down the elusive Philippe, master of the chateau, and she would have all the shots she needed for a stunning photographic essay that would ensure her for the coveted staff position at La Revue.

But soon Britt is swept away by her irresistible attraction to Philippe. Even the painful knowledge of his engagement cannot bridle her errant heart. Suddenly, La Revue seems less important than the Loire winds that had fortuitously blown Philippe to her. Now happiness seems as close as his warm embrace — and as far away as the stars shining in the Mediterranean sky.

SILHOUETTE BOOKS

Another very special love story from Silhouette

GOLDEN TIDE: Sondra Stanford

ONLY FOOLS PLAY WITH FIRE TWICE

Five years ago Melody Travers had fled in humiliation and anger from her marriage to Brand Travers. He was a hard man used to making decisions and having them instantly obeyed. Now he was forcing her to marry him again, but was it revenge that he wanted?

She might have saved her brother from a prison sentence but her own term was going to be much more difficult to serve. Would hate be more binding than love, or would Melody be able to reignite the long-dormant flame of passion in Brand's heart?

She would have to try for herself and for the child she carried.

SILHOUETTE BOOKS

Silhouette Romance

THE NEW NAME IN LOVE STORIES

If you have enjoyed this book, you will want to read the other exciting romances published this month:

SHADOW AND SUN by Mary Carroll
Britt Ryan, a budding photographer, can't get over her anger at Philippe Dolman, whose refusal to meet her may cost her her job at the prestigious *La Revue*. But then she meets Philippe — and her anger is all but forgotten under his sensuous spell.

AFFAIRS OF THE HEART by Nora Powers
Photographer Jess Stanton has been hired by wealthy Derek Thorpe as part of a jungle expedition. But Derek is angry; he had expected a man. Can Jess make him glad she's a woman?

STORMY MASQUERADE by Anne Hampson
Karen Waring was an actress playing her most difficult role: a middle-aged housekeeper working for playwright Clint Fraser. Then, one night, Clint accidentally met the real Karen, and suddenly she didn't know who she was — or who she wanted to be.

PATH OF DESIRE by Ellen Goforth
When Megan Taylor goes to Panama, she expects only to have a job with a prestigious charity drive, but then she meets handsome Jacques Ducruet and is suddenly embarked on a totally unexpected romance.

GOLDEN TIDE by Sondra Stanford
Five years ago, Melody Travers divorced her husband Brand without an explanation. Now he has forced her to become his wife again — and reawakened the passions she had tried to forget.

MIDSUMMER BRIDE by Mary Lewis
Eve Tremaine is in Sweden for a vacation when she meets fiery Max, Count von Sternja. The two soon fall deeply in love, but he must marry her cousin or call down a curse that has hung over her family for centuries.

CAPTIVE HEART by Patti Beckman
JoNell Carpenter is an experienced pilot, so she is understandably insulted when Jorge Del Toro refuses to accept her as his flight instructor. But she is even more insulted when he proposes marriage.

PAYMENT IN FULL by Anne Hampson
Sarah Holmes had once refused Carl Duris' proposal of marriage but now, with no choice in the matter, she has become his wife. At first an unwilling prisoner on his island she is soon held captive not by Carl, but by the demands of her own foolish heart.

Silhouette **Romance**

THE NEW NAME IN LOVE STORIES

Six new titles every month bring you the best in romance. Set all over the world, here are six exciting and brand new stories about people falling in love:

BRIDGE OF LOVE by Lesley Caine
Beth Jackson has gone to India to buy clothes for the boutique that employs her. But the search for an heirloom wedding dress introduces her to Karim Singh — and to a love beyond her wildest dreams.

AWAKEN THE HEART by Dorothy Vernon
A job in an antique store, surrounded by treasures of the past, turns up something new for Abigail Forrest. Her magnetic employer Guy Anderson, is the man of her dreams — but her stepmother once dreamed of him too.

UNREASONABLE SUMMER by Dixie Browning
Emily Fairchild has rented a North Carolina beach house, intending to get away from all the pressures of her life. But when she finds Brandon George living in the other half of the cottage, the battle is on — and Emily's heart is the prize.

PLAYING FOR KEEPS by Brooke Hastings
Nikki Warren had only answered Michael Cragun's ad as a joke. After all, who would want to have a stranger's baby? But now Michael isn't a stranger anymore — and Nikki's heart is no longer her own.

RED, RED ROSE by Tess Oliver
Gardener Sarah Halston is hired to landscape Kight Ramsey's California mansion. At first she wants to be treated as a fellow professional, but she soon wants more. Will Kight ever realize that she's a woman?

SEA GYPSY by Fern Michaels
Cathy Bissette is thrilled to be the editor of seagoing writer Teak Helm. But he is a difficult man to work with, almost as difficult as Jared Parsons, the man who sails into her heart.

Silhouette Romance

EXCITING MEN,
EXOTIC PLACES, HAPPY ENDINGS . . .

Contemporary romances for today's woman

If there's room in your life for a little more romance,
SILHOUETTE ROMANCES are for you.

And you won't want to miss a single one so start
your collection now.

Look for them wherever books are sold
or order from the coupon below.

No. 1	THE DAWN STEALS SOFTLY Anne Hampson		
		65p	26404 7
No. 2	SHADOW AND SUN Mary Carroll	65p	25999 X
No. 3	AFFAIRS OF THE HEART Nora Powers	65p	26000 9
No. 4	STORMY MASQUERADE Anne Hampson	65p	26001 7
No. 5	PATH OF DESIRE Ellen Goforth	65p	26002 5
No. 6	GOLDEN TIDE Sondra Stanford	65p	26003 3
No. 7	MIDSUMMER BRIDE Mary Lewis	65p	26004 1
No. 8	CAPTIVE HEART Patti Beckman	65p	26005 X

**All these books are available at your local bookshop or
newsagent, or can be ordered direct from the publisher. Just
tick the titles you want and fill in the form below.**

Prices and availability subject to change without notice.

SILHOUETTE BOOKS, P.O. Box 11, Falmouth, Cornwall.

Please send cheque or postal order, and allow the following for
postage and packing:

U.K. — One book 30p, 15p for the second book plus 12p for
each additional book ordered, up to a maximum of £1.29.

B.F.P.O. and EIRE — 30p for the first book, 15p for the
second book plus 12p per copy for the next 7 books; thereafter
6p per book.

OTHER OVERSEAS CUSTOMERS — 50p for the first book
plus 15p per copy for each additional book.

Name ....

Address...

....